C000046379

Galway Then, Galway Now

Crannóg 2020 Anthology

ISBN 978-1-907017-57-5

Cover images: 'Long Walk' by Patricia Burke Brogan. 'Quay Street' by Wordsonthestreet.
Cover design: Wordsonthestreet
Published by Wordsonthestreet for Crannóg magazine   @CrannogM

Crannóg Editorial Board: Sandra Bunting, Ger Burke, Jarlath Fahy, Tony O'Dwyer

Comhairle Cathrach na Gaillimhe
Galway City Council

MESSAGE FROM PRESIDENT MICHAEL D. HIGGINS

Publishing 52 issues of Crannóg, offering 18 years of Galway writing to the wider public is a significant achievement. To do so now in Covid conditions is a truly wonderful response and how appropriate it is to have Patricia Burke Brogan's painting on the cover. Patricia who was from the beginning as artist and advocate responsible for so much in Galway's cultural life and continues with her love and belief in the importance of the arts.

I wish all those involved in Crannóg, which offers so much to the literary life of our society, every success as they continue their important work.

Michael D. Higgins
Uachtarán na hÉireann
President of Ireland

CONTENTS

A Reckoning

Kevin Higgins

after Christina Rosetti

My lungs are an accordion fallen out of tune
playing an air I've grown too used to.
Pour me tall glass after tall glass of summer sea air;
let me gulp them down with sliced strawberries.
My lungs belong in a shop
that sells second-hand bagpipes to the gullible.
May the cigarette smoke and diesel fumes of others
(and the mould and stress I brought to the table myself)
all be detained in the lamp-lit interrogation room
I'm building without planning permission
at the bottom of the garden.

My lungs are two talentless divas
competing with each other for newspaper headlines.
May everyone be arrested without warrant
and made plead.
Because the bill for my life is on the mat.
My lungs are rooms in which the yellow
wallpaper is slowly falling down.
My hates have come to get me
and are busy printing the word guilty on every
piece of paper they can find.

From Crannóg 51

At the Grave of Kate O'Brien (1897 – 1974)

Joan McBreen

In Faversham, Kent on a bitter April day,
restless birds of sorrow fly over
the wet stones and grass.
Three times we walk among the paths
and graves and cannot find yours.

Is your only need now the sway of trees
and secret meetings with tufts of time?
But we have travelled far to leave here
without bringing you one spray
of thyme and mock orange blossom.

A sudden downpour, pierced
by shafts of sleet. We stumble
on your headstone. It leans to one side
in all its brokenness.
Spring loneliness. One crow flies into the sky.

From Crannóg 31

The Stillness of the World Before Bach

Lars Gustaffsson

Version by Eva Bourke

There must have been a world before the trio sonata in D,
a world before the A minor partita,
but what kind of a world?
A Europe of vast empty spaces without resonance
everywhere unenlightened instruments
whose keys were neither touched
by the Musical Offering nor the Well-Tempered Clavier.
Remote lonely churches
where no soprano voice from the St Matthew's Passion
intertwined in grief-stricken love
with the gentler phrases of the flute,
wide serene landscapes
where silence reigned but for the old woodcutters' axes
and the cheerful barking of healthy dogs in winter
and, like a bell, skates cutting into glistening ice;
swallows whirring through summer air,
the snail shell held up to the child 's ear
and nowhere Bach
nowhere Bach,
the ice-skater's stillness of the world before Bach.

From Crannóg 31

A Fruit Machine Named Jude

Hugo Kelly

During the long nights of her illness Mrs Moran often thought about her days running the Tea Cosy Café. She would think of Bernie, Madge Grimes and Mrs J., all her old friends playing Jude, their beloved fruit machine, in the warm fug of steam and cigarette smoke while outside night fell upon the quiet streets of the small town. These memories helped her in the empty hours when Death patrolled the silent corridors of the hospital. She would see his shadow blocking the fissure of light that seeped in from the corridor and she would hold her breath until it sloped away from the door. In time dawn would bring relief.

The other women that shared the small ward though were not happy. They complained to the nurses, saying that Mrs Moran was frightening them calling out in the middle of the night about death and a strange man called Jude. So one Friday she was moved to a private room and there she waited for the upcoming night in trepidation, praying deeply until she fell asleep.

She woke many hours later in her shadowed room. Immediately she recognised the shuffling on the corridor as Death made his rounds. She pressed the morphine pump but it did no good. The slouching became louder. She called out but no one heard her. The door of the room swung open and from the corner of her eye she could see Death standing there, a stain upon the darkness.

'Go away. I'm not ready,' she whispered.

Suddenly the room brightened and she sensed change, a strange transformation that she could not explain. She raised herself in the bed and saw to her delight that many elements of the Tea Cosy had emerged magically from the long shadows of the room. The steel kettle gleamed and hummed behind the long Formica counter and the high stools. In the corner the jukebox clicked and she inhaled the oily warmth of the kerosene heater that glowed from the far wall. Beside her, the stout figure of Jude played out its electronic rhythms of light and sound.

Then on her left, the door to the ensuite opened and she gave a little cry of happiness as three figures emerged and she recognised her old friends, Bernie, Mrs J. and Madge Grimes. They smiled kindly at Mrs Moran and then in unison turned to view Death who still stood in the doorway, eyeing him like he was the source of a bad draught.

'Clear off you and leave a poor sick woman alone. And her a widow as well,' Bernie said.

'Yes,' said Mrs J. 'Get away you dirty thing.'

Death studied them intently and then as if judging that their combined strength was too much shook his head and shuffled away down the corridor searching for another victim.

The women took their usual seats at the counter.

'That will soften his cough,' said Madge Grimes.

'He will be back but we're grand for the moment,' Bernie said.

She leaned forward and rubbed the back of Mrs Moran's hands.

'Well,' she said, 'it's good to see you. You're looking well considering. Isn't she looking well girls?'

'Younger you're getting,' said Mrs J.

'I've always envied your skin,' Madge Grimes said, which Mrs Moran knew was a lie.

Still she stared at them in wonder. It had been a long time since they had been together like this. Their relationships had never been the same once she had closed the Tea Cosy. One by one they had passed on: she was the last of them left.

'I've been better,' she said.

Madge Grimes had stood up and was filling a number of cups of tea from the kettle behind the counter. Carefully she handed them around to the others.

'I must say this is a very nice place,' she said. Then the level of her voice fell a notch. 'Though there does seem to be a lot of them...*foreign doctors*...about.'

'Some of them look very handsome to me,' Bernie said. 'I wouldn't mind. I wouldn't mind at all.'

'They charge for parking outside,' Mrs Moran said.

'They do *what*?' Madge Grimes interjected. 'At a hospital!'

'I wouldn't give it to them. I'd park at the University and just walk across,' Mrs J. said.

'They clamp there too these days.'

The women shook their heads and sipped their mugs of tea.

Madge Grimes opened her bag and took out a pack of Carroll's cigarettes. She fitted the plastic filter that she always used to the cigarette and then carefully lit it with her lighter. She sucked deeply, rolling the smoke out of her mouth.

'God,' she says, 'you don't know how long I've been longing to have one of these.'

She flicked the ash onto the floor as she always had done. It still annoyed Mrs Moran but she didn't say anything. Madge Grimes could give you an awful wipe if she wanted.

Mrs J. stood up from the high stool and slotted a ten pence piece into Jude and stroked the play bar like it was an afterthought. The machine ticked into life, the reels spinning, the lights flicking across its brow revealing images of gold coins and pounds signs and overflowing treasure chests. The reels came to a stop. Three cherries in a row. Jude gave a shudder and Mrs Moran sensed the silent urging of the women as if the machine was been coaxed to make its offering. And then sure enough came the scrape of coins falling as Jude tossed out the five ten pence pieces.

'Ah Jude you're being generous tonight,' Mrs J. said.

'Sure isn't it in his nature,' said Madge Grimes, laughing.

Mrs Moran sipped from the mug of tea. It was good to have people around. For much of her life she had been lonely. Francie, her husband, had gone to England for work. He had died in an accident, building the M6 motorway. She had been a widow at thirty five years of age. It was Bernie who had suggested opening up a small café in the front of the house. It had been her big adventure, selling teas and cakes and toasted sandwiches to the lads working in the textiles or the passing girls on their way to the hat factory.

It was Mrs Grime's turn to put a coin into Jude. They eagerly awaited the play and it seemed easier to talk now that their concentration was elsewhere.

Mrs Moran cleared her throat.

'I had to sell the house to pay for the bills. A developer bought it. Knocked it and half of Princess Street to the ground. The Tea Cosy is gone forever.'

Jude's reels ticked to a halt. No win. Madge Grimes sighed to herself and pressed the play bar again. The reels began to spin on the second play.

'Bricks and mortar. That's all it was,' Bernie said. 'It's the memories that matter.'

It was true Mrs Moran thought. So much conversation had taken place in the Tea Cosy. The place had been a refuge from the difficulties of their homes and marriages and diminished dreams. And if they couldn't mend each others lives then they had diluted the pain with tea and biscuits and conversation and Jude's spinning reels. Those few years had been the happiest of her life she realised. Before the hat factory closed and the girls left for Dublin or London or New York. Before the Guards came to take Jude away after someone complained that it was breaking the law.

The reels had come to a halt. No win this time either.

'I miss you all,' she said. 'I really do.'

She felt a stab of emotion like a finger probing her heart. A thin tear ran from the corner of her eyes. She cried for the pain in her bones. She cried for the husband that she had barely known. The emotion drained her and she closed her eyes. Sleep seemed so tempting but she felt a sudden coldness that made her gasp. She opened her eyes and her heart cried out when she saw that Death had entered the room.

'Shush it's alright,' Bernie said. 'Just trust us and it will be alright.'

And it was true that Death's attentions seemed elsewhere. He had taken hold of Jude and with great strength was nimbly moving the machine in a rocking motion, corner by corner to the door of the room. Speckles of light, like the stars gleaming in the night sky, were sprinkled across his dark shape. John Denver was playing on the jukebox and the notes gushed all around them, filling the room with prairie warmth. And as she stared it seemed to Mrs Moran that Death and Jude were waltzing across the floor in a tender embrace, a strange but wonderful dance that filled her with confusion and yet a strange calm. She was moving beyond regret and fear. The difficulties of her life lost their edge within her memory and became the incidents of an existence, the ticking of reels, aligning themselves in so many possible combinations. She felt a lightness of being. Something was being discarded, being left behind. The sickness that had eaten her very core was evaporating away to nothing.

Mrs. J. and Madge Grimes stood up. Madge Grimes took a few quick pulls of the cigarette, sucking it into herself, before stubbing it out on the ground.

'Didn't I enjoy that?' she said to no one in particular.

Mrs J. rubbed her clothes down and searched in her bag for a comb and her pink compact. Bernie offered her hand to Mrs Moran.

'It's time to go,' she said.

'Yes,' said Mrs Moran, 'No point putting it off any longer.'

She found as she swung her legs that they had unexpected strength and she slipped out from underneath the sheets and onto the warm tiles. Bernie took her hand and gently swaying to the music, the women followed Death as it guided Jude out of the room.

Now Mrs Moran saw that they were not in the corridor but were on Princess Street and Death was manoeuvring Jude through the tight door of the Tea Cosy. Bernie, Mrs J. and Madge Grimes followed him in but she stood in the middle of the street. It was as she remembered it. The small houses and the few shops leaned into the hill behind. The yellow beams of the streetlights shivered against the shadows. A mist was washing in from the sea and it gently wet her face and after the stale air of the hospital it felt rich and vital. Corcoran's free hanging sign across the road was rattling and there was the shunting groan of the nine o'clock train arriving from

Dublin. The lights of the Tea Cosy shone out brashly through the condensation covered windows. The door opened and Death emerged back onto the street. He winked at her as he passed and continued on his journey up the town. Through the half opened door Mrs Moran could hear much talking and laughter coming from inside. The women were sitting in the fug of smoke and sweet tea paying occasional attention to the gurgling voice of Jude as it shimmered beneath the crackling fluorescent light.

Bernie suddenly stuck her head out the door.

'Would you ever come in? You'll be drenched out there.'

'I'm coming,' said Mrs Moran, pushing the door open. She was home and there were a thousand things to do before tomorrow came.

From Crannóg 28

Fifteen
Ed Boyne

That summer, jokers, kings and aces were stripped out.
The deck was scanned for slynesses, fresh treacheries.

We ground coffee, learned the lore of beers.
Desire came fast, was under-stated, then swollen.

The music needed darkness, the scent of hair, those moments
tense as fag drags, the length of three slow tracks.

Smoke identified the air, its meaning full to the chest.
We sucked the frantic present in and held it.

Laughter shaped the walls, made the ceiling buckle.
Certainty was a mirror, a back-combed fringe.

In those kept weeks we warmed the one wood floor.
I feel it supple still, humming, under my toes.

From Crannóg 33

Being Gaia
Elizabeth Power

His/story cleared the practice of sacred from the earth.
I see her red dance of heat. Inside she burns at the betrayal.
To lose and know that lose so profoundly.
Weak from the force of an enemy more skilled in plunder
She looks dismayed at her body, her skin torn
Her seas, her waters running in currents of sewerage
'Man,' she wheezes through a phosphorescent fog
'Your shit will kill me.'

From Crannóg 50

Aubade
Clare Sawtell

June 21st 2018

There's a branch in the wood
where the sun never shines
except this day.
It's moving slowly in the morning.
I can just see it
through the trees.

MRI scan this afternoon.
Magpies have such beautiful wings
when they're outstretched.

May what needs to be seen be
seen and what doesn't
remain uncovered.

From Crannóg 49

Bicycle Ride

Pat Mullan

I sat on the cold handlebars
my thighs bone-tight to the metal
as you pushed me

Your breath spluttered
hot on my neck
like the engine in
your old Morris Minor

Up and up that brae
you pushed till you seemed
to stand still on the pedals
almost waiting to fall

Hailstones beat down
on my bare legs
till they were scourged red
but I don't remember the pain

I only remember your strength
and your closeness.
We were never like that again.

From Crannóg 34

Cartography

Luke Morgan

They begin the intricate act of pin-
pointing the surface of your skin into
a 2-D, immovable country on the monitor
where the psychedelic colours
of the body's temperatures and breathing motions
could be a weather forecast or an elevation study.

Tracing the region borders between nape
and collar-bone, shoulder and ulna,
they find what they're looking for North,
a few kilometres-to-scale
below of the jawline straight as a continent-
edge;

a raised hub of land, hard as moss-covered flint,
and with tools that can be likened
to rulers, brass compasses, pencils
sharpened to scalpel-tips,
they mark it with an "X",
begin planning the dig

while I struggle at reading their chart,
no wiser than I ever was
at understanding the map
of your road systems, tiny estuaries –
not knowing which way is up or down,
East, West.

From Crannóg 35

August in Memoriam

Caitlyn Rooke

Hands, chilled with day's close, comb through silted locks while
the decades worn towel wrapped around falls to sand-dusted toes.
Pruned fingertips check the elastic round my waist as I leave
fire's confines, throwing warmth over for the motion of stillness.

I hop from soft to soft above smooth stones, slowing only as toes taste
water's ebb. I don't linger on his not quite scattered ashes in the shallows.
But I note their fine white paleness against the coarse ochres
of our shore, a transient monument for the ashes which still glow.

I cut around this life under glass and into the water until the rounded
part of my belly sits below the line and I imagine I'm slim like sixteen.
I know I'll go under but I don't think of it as I slip down. Eyelids resting
together, I know light and dark by their coldness and warmth.

And with arced back I rise to see the sun's belly on the line,
its pinkness blooming into the water with no thought.

From Crannóg 48

The Lost Girls
Celeste Augé

The myth of home carried her
through the maze of towering pines
on the edge of a paper town,
past Wawa, Blind River, Webbwood,
through bewildered years of motherhood,
three house moves within thirty miles
and the unfamiliar life of a wife.

The allure of that myth, of
'*I'll take you home again Kathleen*'
played on her radio again and again,
the pull of that lyric so strong
she flew over the ocean to a home
where she no longer spoke the language.

The pull of home so strong she gathered
what was precious into the night:
three girls, with enough life between them
to tiptoe the beach for live crabs and jellyfish.
Tucked the three things she'd learnt
into the pouch on her back and flew
clear across the Atlantic Ocean,
geography stripping back with each mile,
creating a brood of wayless daughters.

From Crannóg 19

Corps de Ballet
James Martyn Joyce

When you said that with his legs,
my grandson could be a ballet dancer,
I saw graves open on the low slope
of the New Cemetery,
ancestors grip the clay edge,
bone hands hauling them up,
heard them snap pale fingers,
rattle knuckles on bare ribs,
before skipping, childlike, downhill,
arm in bleached arm, bony knees askew,
fixed grins on their chalk faces,
their fleshless mouths struggling,
stumbling the words:
tombé, plié, pas-de-deux.

From Crannóg 44

Wave
Connnie Masterson

Dressed in layers
of silk scarves
you dance
arms outstretched
with wings of coloured silk
that quiver like fins -
the kitchen, suddenly,
transformed into
an exotic aquarium;
entranced, we follow
your flitting performance.

And perhaps,
on the eve of the Epiphany,
a visit from one of the three
bearing golden moments,
pure essence
or mermaid's mirror.

While the natural world brings
its tidal wave of sorrow, joy
breaks through with your
splendid Angel Fish dance.

From Crannóg 9

Poetic Justice

Moya Roddy

Fuckin' mad, Stacey thought, staring at the crowd gathered in front of the building opposite. Imagine goin' to hear fuckin' poetry this hour of the morning. A red banner blazed across the entrance: *Cúirt International Festival of Poetry and Literature*. 'Cúirt' had a fada. What did it mean? Something to do with courting? Isn't that what her granny told her they used to call kissing? Having a good court, except she pronounced it curt. Not that Stacey could imagine her granny kissing anyone. Or anyone kissing her granny. No one with eyesight anyway. Still she must have and more, otherwise her ma wouldn't be here. And if her ma wasn't here she wouldn't be standing outside a poxy courthouse waiting for her case to be called. Her granny shoulda kept her tongue to herself.

Stacey shook out a cigarette, lit up. Across the road it was mostly women, one girl her own age chatting up a gink with glasses. What kind of poetry do you like? Up me hole! Cunts, the lot of them. Going to a fuckin' poetry reading and she was up for stealing a bloody hair straightener. Top of the range though, she'd been hoping to sell it to her sister-in-law whose hair frizzed just from people sneezing. Would ye look at them, gab, gab, gab. No one this side was talkin. Except the barristers and solicitors and they were only talking to themselves.

I could be over there, I used to like poetry at school. When I went. Shite! I'll be feeling sorry for myself in a minute. Where the fuck is- She looked round, saw him coming, like a giant bat. Hair and spit flying.

'Stacey, sorry, I got caught up in Court 2. You won't be called before 12.30. I had a word with the magistrate.'

'Fuck! What am I supposed to do? Hang round this dump for another coupla hours?'

'You could go into town, I suppose.' He looked at her sharply. 'If you do any shopping, remember to pay for it!'

Stacey gave him the finger. Not that she minded. Dennis was alright. Mostly.

'Fuck off.'

'Sorry. Better go. 12. 30. Here. Don't be late.'

'You sound like my mother.'

Stubbing out her fag, Stacey watched him rush back in, gown ballooning, documents slipping from his arms.

Asshole, she thought, going down the steps. Opposite, people had begun to drift in. Stacey crossed the road towards them, sure everyone was watching her.

Relax, I'm not coming to steal your bags. Not today anyway.

Stupid cows, she liked the thought of putting them on edge.

From inside the building a buzzer sounded. Stacey hovered at the bottom of the steps, awkward.

'It'll be starting soon,' a woman nudged her.

'I'm not going in.'

'Might be good. It's free.'

Stacey shrugged.

The woman smiled, pushed in a door, disappeared. Stacey stared after her, stared back at the court, at the traffic lights changing to red.

Cheaper than a cup of coffee, Stacey decided, attaching herself to the tail end of the crowd, her eyes pinned to the ground. Besides, she might bump into Ryan up town. Cunt. Didn't even turn up this morning and she'd asked him. Told him anyway. Just as well. Great impression he'd make on the judge.

The warmth hit her as she slid into a seat near the exit. She could always do a runner if it was bollix. Around her, mouths opened and shut like the goldfish in her granny's flat. She heard a crackling then a voice erupted from a speaker. Stacey listened to the usual warnings about exits and entrances, about taking photos, turning off mobiles. When the announcement finished there was silence, a feeling of expectation. A man ambled onto the stage.

'You're welcome,' he beamed, 'to this year's twenty-second annual Cúirt Festival ...'

Stacey's fingers tapped her thigh, the armrest. She felt trapped. Like in a cell. She watched others clapping, the sound increasing as a woman appeared, slight, nervous looking. Like the woman that time. The one she'd robbed. Shook all over she had, handing over the purse. Stacey hadn't meant to scream at her. The way the woman reacted made her.

The woman on stage bowed, smiled. 'Thank you. Thank you. I'm delighted to be here.' The papers in her hand trembled.

Stacey wondered what it must be like to walk out on stage, have people clap you. All those eyes. She'd die. Like being in the school play, only worse. Not that she'd ever been in it. Never been asked.

The woman fumbled, began to read.

Fuck, she hasn't even learned it. Stacey checked to see if anyone minded but no one seemed to notice. Signs on, she hadn't gone to her school. Sister Agnes wouldn't stand for that. The poem was over in a flash. Only a few people clapped and Stacey felt sorry for the woman. When she began another poem Stacey realised she hadn't heard a word of the first. She couldn't listen. She wasn't in the mood.

Stacey closed her eyes, heavy from the heat. The woman's voice had a kind of rhythm or maybe the words had: Stacey felt her body relax, settle, the rush of blood slow. God, she was tired. Tired, fucking, tired. The voice grew fainter, vanished.

Stacey woke with a start. People were standing, putting on coats. Fuck, what time was it? She pulled out her mobile. Twelve twenty-five, she was alright.

Dennis was on the steps. He screwed up his eyebrows seeing her come out of the theatre.

'I didn't know you liked poetry?'

'Don't. It's crap. Are we going in?"

'We've got ten minutes. So it wasn't any good, the reading?'

'I fell asleep.'

He looked at her, the way guards did when they want you to incriminate yourself.

'OK, I used like it at school. One poem anyway. Can't remember, something about going into a wood.' She knew the words off by heart - Sister Agnes had make sure of that - but she wasn't going to tell him.

'Was it Yeats? *Song of the Wandering Aengus*?'

'Dunno.'

'"I went into a hazel wood, because a fire was in my head-"'

'That's it,' Stacey interrupted. She didn't want him knowing it.

'What did you like about it?'

'Dunno. How I feel sometimes. There a fuckin' like fire in me head.'

She shouldn't be telling him this. Told him too much, already.

'What do you mean?'

'Nothin' just mouthin'. Listen, you gotta get me off. I can't go down. It'll kill my mother. You won't see me here again. Promise.'

'You said that last time. And there's your previous.'

'I didn't mean it before. I do, now. I got a

boyfriend Ryan, we're gonna like, get a place together.'

'Tell me about the poem? The fire in your head.'

'What for? It's like nothin', like seeing red ..' She picked at the skin round her thumb.

'Is that what happens,' he pursued, 'before you take something, you see red?'

'Dunno. Sometimes. You'll get me off, won't ye?'

'I'll try. Behave yourself in there, no temper.'

Stacey listened to the proceedings, trying not to catch the judge's eye. Fuckin' woman magistrate, the worst. Feel they have to punish you.

Dennis sat down at the end of his plea, glanced over at her, stood up again.

'Might I request that this case be adjourned for reports?'

The magistrate sniffed. 'I don't see any need for reports. Young lady, you are a disgrace.'

'Your honour. I think ... My client gave me some new information .. which may have some bearing.

'What sort of information?'

'I wonder if we could adjourn for a psychiatric report. You see my client told me that before she commits a crime, that, as she put it, her head goes on fire, she sees red-'

'What the fuck-' Stacey screamed.

'Young lady, one more sound out of you-'

'That was fuckin' private, dickhead! What you doing telling the whole fucking world!' Stacey stared, her heart thumping, the room already turning.

The magistrate banged the table. 'I warned you.'

'I'm not fuckin' mad, I'd rather go to fuckin' prison.'

'That's precisely where you are going. I sentence Stacey O'Connor to one month. Leave to appeal is withheld.'

'Bastard,' Stacey shouted at Dennis as they led her away, 'fuckin' bastard.'

From Crannóg 19

Daedalus Speaks To Icarus, His Son
Liz Quirke

How it is that I who can coax stone
into labyrinthine detail could fail
to build the basics of your senses?

My greatest success stands as a reliquary
to forever keep what little was gathered of you,
your robe, splinters of your bones,

slivers of pride among scattered, waxless feathers,
fingertips still reaching towards the sky.

My son, you surrendered to the vanity
of a daring death, tested yourself
in elemental ways you were not born to conquer.

No Apollo you, what was your last thought?
Did you call Father into the wind as you fell?

Or did the arrogance that the next upward gust was yours
keep you silent as the water rushed to fill your mouth?

The women say their mothering ears still hear your cries,
their night-feed hearts slowed to a dimming thrum

when you failed to breach the surface.
They detailed in that way of women
how it feels to see a child's body broken,

because you were child to them,
and they can cry for you and remember
your newborn skull warm in the palm of their hand.

From Crannóg 43

Dragon Pearls
Majella Kelly

for Frank

...your smell was never unfamiliar.
                    Rebecca Perry

It's the third Wednesday in February
and I'm waiting upstairs in a café
at six o'clock, with a cup of jasmine
tea. It's our first meeting, and I wonder
could a plant be romantic? Jasmine might,
snow-white blossoms spoon-tight at sunrise;
that gasp of petals as they part in the dark
which signals a readiness for scenting:
the layering of green tea buds and leaves
the tea master has kept since April to be
mated, night after night, for the perfect blend,
then hand-rolled into tiny, silken pillows
he calls dragon pearls. You offer your hand
– it is exactly the right temperature.

From Crannóg 41

Fatal Distraction
Pete Mullineaux

No, I can't recollect the place or name –
did I miss something happening there?
The inter-city would have shot on

through, unless ... possibly a signal fault,
some other delay? Then I might have sat
along with the rest, tapping my fingers –

buried in a laptop, crossword, steamy
novel or magazine – attempt at recall
would be in vain, although, no doubt

there would have been identifiable
features; local foliage, background hiss
of wildlife or the human kind.

Now isn't the world insane! And yes –
sorry too I can't be more useful
as a witness. A crime did you say?

From Crannóg 40

Falling Down

Orla Higgins

It's the same dream as before. The one where she and Joe are drinking tea from giant, pink Alice in Wonderland cups they have to hold up with both hands. Her legs are twisted around his as they half-sit, half-lie on her grandmother's green tartan picnic blanket at Ocean Beach. The sound is turned down but they are laughing and spilling tea and then laughing at spilling tea. A red and white polka dot umbrella protects them from the sun while Marcel Marceau performs a private show for their eyes only. He is Joe's favourite mime artist but only because he doesn't know any others.

Jade's eyes flicker open and see nothing but black. She shuts them again waiting for something to register. She waits but there is just a vague realisation that she isn't meant to be lying here on damp, cold concrete ground. Something makes her think she has fallen and she tries to shift her limbs around to see if anything is broken. She's sure she has seen people do this in films. Her right leg is bent under the weight of the left. Both arms are splayed on either side of her body and her neck is twisted in a funny direction to the left. Slowly moving bits and pieces of herself she completes a mental check-list to see if everything is present and correct. Stale dusty air hovers around her nostrils and she wonders if her new skirt is torn. Her arm starts to make its way down towards her leg to find out but it gives up half way there and resorts to lying limply across her stomach. She feels numb.

Jade, she thinks to herself, you have to get up, find out where you are. Jade. The name everyone thinks is so exotic but is really only the result of an atrocious handwriting mistake by the midwife that filled in her birth registration details. It was supposed to read Jean after the women on the maternal side of her family. When she was younger her mother always tried to call her Jean but Jade always refused to answer to the name. And with no other daughters to right the official wrong, her mother had to accept there would not be another chance to continue the family tradition. Jade smiles as she thinks how much she likes her name. She likes the sound of it when people say it out loud, the images it conjures up in other peoples minds. She thinks her life would have been a bore if she had been called Jean. Then again, if she had been called Jean, perhaps she wouldn't have ended up here.

Moving her head to the right, Jade looks up and becomes aware of two lines of light projecting into the dark from a narrow window high up on the wall. She squints trying to make out where she is but can only see lumpy outlines in the darkness. She realises she doesn't have her glasses. She needs her glasses. She isn't sure how long she has been lying here but, at this stage, thinks she should probably shout for help. She wills her voice to work but her throat contracts and she can only manage a hoarse whimper. The effort makes her drowsy and she closes her eyes. Pictures start to flit around behind the naked lids. A rainy funeral. Attic antiques. A small white house. Ocean spray. It reminds her of...she doesn't know...she can only see glimpses. She can't work out what going on.

Then something rips into her consciousness causing her eyes to jump open. Up until this minute she wasn't aware of feeling anything. Now, her muscles are starting to tighten as she feels sensations returning. Pain sears through her lower body. She doesn't know what it feels like to be stabbed but thinks the feeling can't be too far removed from this. Jade feels hot, cold, sick, faint, everything together. She wants to find her glasses and she wants to cry. Her theory about movies and checking limbs seems stupid to her now. The pain tells her she must be broken. She must be broken in many places. It becomes almost beyond her to tolerate the pain but there is nothing else she can do.

She tries to call help again but it doesn't work. It doesn't do anything for the torturous hurt and it doesn't bring rescue. When she tries to move her right leg out from under her left, the pain sends excruciating volts of agony through her body. She is afraid to take anything other than shallow breaths and squeezes her eyes shut trying to remember something good. Maybe if she thinks happy thoughts it will help. Happy thoughts, Jade, there's got to be a life time of them in there. She settles on Granny Jean's rose garden. She loved the sweet smell and the peony petals that trailed around the outside of the house through the higgledy piggledy garden and back to the side porch.

Jade thinks about how she used to sit out there on the porch with *Ballet Shoes*, her favourite book, when she was told to keep out of the way. Keeping out of the way meant avoiding Uncle Tom. He went on the war-path once a week when he got rent from his tenants and blew it all in one monstrous whiskey binge. She tried to shake away his ravaged beard from her memory. Something else now. Another rose garden. From her favourite class. From English. *Footfalls ... down the passage we didn't take ... . toward the door we never opened into the rose garden.* Something like that. She can't remember the full verse. This isn't happy. Those lines always make her sad. Jade shivers, tries to

13

move to get more comfortable and is rewarded again with the prize of pain.

Tears spill and her memory starts to return. She remembers a train journey, a coffin, not feeling sad when she knows she should have been. She thinks for sure she was up there somewhere and now she is down here. It all seems like so long ago, but how long was it? Searching, she remembers an open trap-door. Did she come through it? It must be fifteen feet up to the roof over her head. She looks up but there is only a faint glow in the gloom. Nothing to indicate anyone is up there trying to save her. The notion is strange to her. It's the first time in her life she wants to be saved and there is no other word to use because the pain is inside her head now and she wants to sleep. Sleep and be saved. Anything but have to tolerate …

Screaming. Someone seems to be screaming her name. She finds a small voice to reply *I'm here, but I can't find my glasses*. The voice shouts back that someone called James is coming. Why does everyone always have to shout, wonders Jade? And who is James?

Rattling then. She is aware of rattling to her left from what sounds like a steel door. Keys, chains, pounding. Is the pounding outside or deep within her head? There are no individual parts of her anymore, they are all just blended pain. Should she be afraid of James? She knew a James once and he was a bully. Or was that a Jean? She doesn't care anymore. She wants the door to open, the rattling to stop, the pain to go away. She just wants to be back in the white house by the ocean.

The door crashes open. Bright light splits through the dark and she sees a man dragging a black case with him. He stands over her. Jade presumes it is James even though he doesn't look familiar to her. He thrusts a syringe into a tiny glass tube and empties the contents into her leg, straight through her new skirt. She thinks he's smiling at her but she can't be sure. Something flows through her veins. She recognises him, but it's too late. Jade feels rushing relief. Then floating. Then nothing.

From Crannóg 19

Intrusion
Ger Hanberry

The voice on the phone wore a uniform.
No burglar alarm? Foolish in this day and age.

The crude boot of trespass,
the air smudged and quivering,

drawers left hanging
like the tongues of dead cattle.

You smile bravely
but I watch you walk the house

trying not to caress what had been pawed.
You stop by the empty sideboard,

two vague circles like stamps on an old passport
where our figurines had poised for years,

intact in their elegant world,
a wedding gift,

the slender ballerina stretching high on her tiptoes,
her faithful partner balanced for the clinch.

From Crannóg 8

Navigatio II
StephanieBbrennan

to the lonesomeness
of chant
we stalk awareness
and point
spirit boat
towards summer solstice
west always west
to sit briefly
with Éanna
on shelf of lime-rock
worn by weather
pocked by nostoc
he and the brothers
bright erratics
in sunwise turnings
mussel
whelk
*bairneach**

*limpet

From Crannóg 38

Forecast
Mary Madec

You turn me around and change the frame.
You're sorry and winded.

There's some awkward readjustment of limbs,
like trees that find their branches
when the wind dies down.

We go back the way we came, the cloud breaking up
as it comes in from the sea.

Everything from this angle looks different,
you take out your thermometer,
barometer, wind vane:

The outlook is good, you say:
Cumulonimbus calvus, your favourite,

a sky filled with narrative,
great big faces puffed,
playfully portentous.

You say they will be tipped
with red and gold at sunset.

From Crannóg 28

November
Patricia Burke Brogan

High above our winter-dead hedge,
a rosebud opens its heart,
glows with new hope,
banishes my night-dark.

Meshed in our winter-dead hedge,
a nest of starlings
hums young with music,
burnishes my life.

From Crannóg 32

Grapevine
Bernie Ashe

After Gaius Petronius, translated by Ben Jonson

Wine, a filthy pleasure, and short;
and pause me out of script, I shed
life's woes, to birth some merriment.
Encase glee, a shrine I visit on my
melancholy day, to pray and resurrection seek
if not then to repeat, repeat with
grape and glass until the memory lost,
floats purple in a hint of oak wood
cask. For then to look and see, how
pleasure lost, as time creates each
stained empty glass.

From Crannóg 37

15

I Told You Everything

Mary Wilkinson

My name is Dot. Dot Goggins. I live in the cul-de-sac that faces the old cemetery out on Bracken Road. Our house, my Mam's and mine, is the one with the broken gate. Mam says that's how you can tell our house is the only rental on the road. It's a quiet enough place though and Mam is convinced we live in one of the better estates in this town. I should say I was supposed to be born a David but when I was in the hospital the nurse put a bunch of dots where my name should have been and so Mam called me Dot after that. I don't mind. It could be worse.

Most days I can tell everything that's going to happen to me. Like today. Friday. It's six a.m. and if you look in through the window you will see me lying stretched out on my bed. I'm wearing my school uniform and reading a book about rainbows.

There is so much to learn about rainbows. A rainbow is an arch of colours visible in the sky, caused by the refraction and dispersion of the sun's light by rain or other water droplets in the atmosphere. So there. Most people never even look at rainbows. But that's not my problem. I've just turned fifteen. And I might add that I've had these books for ages. Rainbow facts are vast. Light for instance is the lifeline to a rainbow and don't even think about catching one or finding a crock of gold at the end. It's all illusion.

Anyway back to now. I'm on the bed.

Check.

As always.

Check.

It feels good to be up early and have no one, but you, looking in on my thoughts.

Check.

Now and then I think about my dad. It is always summertime when I do that. Once June arrived Dad would slowly roll up his sleeves and the legs of his pants like he was thinking about taking on the world and after a few weeks of sunshine he'd decide that life was okay. To be tolerated. And if he saw me looking at him from the window of my room he would wave and then point to his white hairy legs as he scrunched his face to meet the sunlight. Straight-up. Like it was something he had come to terms with. He reminded me there and then of the albino rat they had on display at the pet shop on Eyre Street before it closed down. Everybody was going to see that rat. I can still picture him in the small cage with his nervous pink eyes looking out at me and his nose all snively like he had a permanent cold.

You should know, yes you, the watcher through the window, watching me on my bed, that the other lads' say, look at that Dot Goggins, he's a real weirdo. They all hate me.

Maybe it's the glasses. Mam got them on the medical. I know they call me mole.

Blinkers.

Bugger eyes.

Worse.

This light. This light at six thirty a.m. is special because it comes into the room gradually in a sneaky kind of way. You don't notice it immediately if you know what I'm saying. Slow and easy and soft like cotton wool until wham it gets so bright that you'll be sure to be rubbing your eyes they can hurt so much. Mam gets up soon after. Some days she curses more than others and makes a big racket out in the hall. Like right now, she opens the door and she's shouting at me, I can't do this. I cannot do this anymore. When I ask her what she can't do anymore, she says Dot. Just that. Dot.

And then she puts her arms out on either side of her as if she's trying to hold up a great big heavy rock and says,

This.

Dimwit.

This.

You.

Stupid.

Dimwit.

By the time I get to Eurobreak it is close to eight thirty a.m. Paulina is already halfway through sipping her tea. She smiles at me. Paulina is nice. Her hair is blonde and so straight that it looks like it's been ironed out. I asked her once if they have rainbows in Poland and she laughed and said, silly boy Dot. Today she asks me if it's the usual. I nod.

No mayo?

Check.

No mustard?

Check.

One slice of ham?

Check.

One slice of cheese?

Check.

On white?

Check.

Three euro.

Done.

Paulina says have a good day Dot. She says Dot like I'm someone important.

A kaleidoscope is a toy consisting of a tube containing mirrors and pieces of coloured glass or paper whose reflections, yes, reflections produce changing patterns when the tube is rotated. Dad bought me a kaleidoscope when I was eight. It was made of tin with colours of the rainbow painted all around the outside of it. When I shook it the sound was magic. Shh, shh, shh, as if the colours and shapes were talking and trying to get out.

Walking to school is what it must be like to be stuck inside a great big kaleidoscope.

Tall skinny black railings.

Orange rust beginning to form on top.

A lost and found purple glove stuck on a spike.

Pale blue jumper on woman standing at bus stop.

White bobbles on her sleeves.

Grey seagull.

Swoops low.

Flash.

Check.

Bark of tree peeling silver.

The blare of car horns angry red.

Check.

Baby screams from a buggy.

The mam on phone ignores baby.

The baby is all pink.

Icy white stares.

Light.

Check.

Swish, swishy light through railings.

Dark.

Light.

Dark.

Light.

Shadows.

Touch it.

Shh, shh, shh.

Catch the shadows.

No I won't.

Check.

There's no smell today. Must be the way the wind is blowing. Usually the yard stinks of pig.

Because of Baconland. The factory across the river. Most of the lads' Dads' work in Baconland. Neary's Dad is the foreman. Everyone is friends with Neary. He has what they call leadership qualities. That's what Mr. O'Connor said about him in Civics class. We all need to strive to have 'leadership qualities' like our young man Neary. But I don't have to tell you that. You can see.

Right?

Check.

Back to the yard. I suppose you could call it a normal, boring kind of a yard. Standard size for a yard. Basketball hoops missing nets. Rusting. Twisted. No pig smell today.

That's a bonus.

Check.

Pebble-dash wall. That I use to stand up against. And put my hands on and press them into it so eventually the dashed pebbles make marks on my palms. Small indentations. Neary and his team down the other end. Close enough to the outside toilets. Smoking.

Check.

I pretend not to see. Pretend I'm counting the cars passing by out on the road. Try to look as if I'm concentrating. My palms tingle from the pebble-dash marks. I never can tell what day Neary might be in the mood for me. To get his kicks. Use up some of his leadership qualities. Right now he's talking to his followers in a huddle. One of them turns and calls out.

Goggins.

Goggins get on down here. Then they all start.

Goggins. Goggins. Gog. Gins. Gog. Gins.Cha cha cha. Goggins. Gog.Gins. Gog.Gins.Cha cha cha. Clapping and stamping their feet. Jeers gone mad mixed with smelly fingers always poking at themselves. Great fun it is.

Check.

Did you know that echoes are reflections? Echoes occur because some of the sound waves in your shouts reflect off a surface like a well or a canyon. Or even off a pebble-dash wall if the shouts are loud enough. I know that if I walk down there they'll push me around a bit. Call me queer. Say things about Dad. How he disappeared one day. Soon after the money went missing from the safe at Baconland. How when he was last seen he was walking towards the train station. Someone said he was whistling.

Check.

I wait for the buzzer to signal the start of class. Do you see me?

Waiting.

Friday nights Mam and I always go to China Villa for curry and chips. We sit across from each other at one of the small tables and drink coke while we wait for the food. We don't talk. Mam studies her phone and I look out the window at the dark black shiny street. But somehow I always end up watching our reflection in the big glass window. We could be strangers. Just ordinary people in China Villa waiting for our curry and chips. Although I could watch Mam's reflection all night long. Her head bent over her phone and her thick black hair wrapped around her neck like a small animal taking a bit of a sleep for itself.

Check.

Neary comes in with his Dad for a takeaway. Neary waves over at me and smiles. His Dad says nothing. After they leave Mam says, why don't you get to know that young man?

He seems like a nice lad.

Check.

When we get home I go outside to sit on the wall and look back at the house. The night changes everything. Takes the edge off. With a few lights on. An illusion? Maybe.

I see Mam pour a shot out for herself and drink it quickly. Then she pours another one and turns to go down to the room to watch telly. I imagine Dad then outside the kitchen window in his rolled up pants and sleeves. Freckles scattered like huge raisins along his arms as he unravels the hose until it becomes a big yellow snake that stretches the length of the garden. Then Dad slowly turns on the tap. He's telling me we need to do it properly. I remember the water coming out in shy gurgles and sputters until it flowed in a clear, even stream. I remember thinking something special was going to happen.

Check.

And then I'm touching it. The something special was right there in my hands. The yellow of forgiveness. The blue of hope. The red. The orange. All arched in the spray. And Dad reminding me how he said that he'd catch us a rainbow someday. How anything's possible.

Check.

I hear Mam calling me. Dot. Where are you Dot? I decide not to answer her straight away. My voice stays stuck down inside of me. I'm going back over the day. How this very morning I told you I knew everything that would happen to me today. And I did. I told you everything. Well almost everything. There is something else but it might be best not to mention that. Some things can wait. There will always be another opportunity.

Check.

Like reflections that never stop coming. Or echoes like the ones running around in my head.

Echoes that might just get too loud. Then what? Mam's closing the venetian blind now. The slats throw shadows across her body to make her look as if she's in a prison cell.

I whisper Mam.
Wait Mam wait.
What's on the telly Mam?
I'm coming Mam.
Tell me something Mam.
Anything at all Mam.
Do you remember Mam?
Wait Mam.
Wait.
Check.

From Crannóg 50

Lives of the Great Novelists
Alan McMonagle

I am melting from the inside.
Have drunk all my blood;
and while I await the new spleen
put in for several lifetimes ago,
am gradually chewing my way
through my rattling ribcage.
Not much meat on that.
Just a short time ago,
it seems, I was all set to suck
the ocean through a straw.
Now I think my sordid pancreas
might have to see me through.
It's either that or the albino python
I have been babysitting
for my Egyptian friend
who left the country.
Six months ago and counting.

From Crannóg 40

Lone Journey
Marie Coyne

When the moon got up tonight
she came to my feet
and gently washed her face
In rippling lake water,

She dried herself
with passing white clouds
and set sail for ocean night,

Out there all alone
she is making empty silver roads
I wish I could walk upon.

From Crannóg 24

Little Pools of Light
Sandra Bunting

after Leonard Cohen

Sheep then leap to bring on sleep,
the fences are too high.
You shut your eyes and cease to weep,
a simple lullaby,

and on a dark and lonely breeze,
gliding bats begin to fright,
wild eyes look at you from trees.
Little pools of light.

The worm is hidden in the fruit,
crows stab with their beaks,
the apple sticks, makes them mute.
a circus act of freaks.

Back and forth the crash of waves,
decide what you can keep.
Chambered in the mind, it saves
in the place of good sleeps.

But what waits out in the forest dark
or through your inner sight,
by the sea or in the park?
Little pools of light.

Go deep down and meet the child
and ask it what it wants.
It's standing in a river mild,
frightened, small and gaunt.

Look at the one and take its hand.
You recognize its plight.
Walk with it in that murky land
to find little pools of light.

From Crannóg 48

Love is Not a Question
Sighle Meehan

I see you in the hollow where the willow trees
have shed their catkins,
you select a sally rod, shear it of its leaves,
test its whip against the breeze.

In a little while you will come back indoors,
place the rod on a shelf above the cooker
where earlier you seared meat, chopped carrots,
secured the kitchen with the herbal warmth
of beef and kidney casserole.

You dally, distracted by the glut of Summer,
I see you lean into the sunshine, lift
your hand as though to touch
the sea-pinks and chamomile of yesterdays
when you were still a girl, skittish,
unbraced for womanhood.

I hear the grunt of diggers on the widening road,
progress poking through the fences
of my childhood.
You listen for the homing call
of an incoming tide,
sands already spooling out
the bruises of your future.

You see me watching.
I watch now through telescopic years
the vigour in your auburn hair
laughter lines round eyes not yet turned yellow,
you smile, you wave the sally rod,
grow me in the scope of both.

From Crannóg 42

Keeper of Earth

Sandra Coffey

Elsie Barker was the queen of the crossroads. For 35 years and in all kinds of weather, she got the 7am bus to work at the same crossroads. She did quality checks on drip bags for hospitals. She died suddenly at the age of 70.

I got the call and wrote the arrangements in my diary. I knew the plot well, having put her husband down 10 years before. I checked the weather and calculated the best times to get the lads up to start the dig. Rain is the killer. It would have the hole filled up while you'd be walking out of the cemetery, if you didn't watch it. Elsie was going in on top of her husband Aloysius. We'd only a few feet to dig. She was the last to go down in that plot. It was a right cunt of a plot, boggy and wet and I sure was damn glad we'd never have to dig it again.

'Is there enough room?' That's all they want to know. The mourners. They expect the hole to be there when they arrive. They don't want to hear about how it got there, the rock, the rain and anything else.

'Don't let anything get in the way; he has to go down there,' said Margaret Potts, the time she was burying her brother. Plots are expensive. At least 6K.

You wouldn't want to know what we've come across during a dig. I'll tell you about one time to give you an idea. It was one of those summer days when all you wanted was to sit on a wall with a Choc Ice in your hand. But, there we were digging, and the sweat running off our sun-blocked skin. We dug down as far as we could with the mini digger. Then we got the shovels and after that it's a case of judging where the coffins are.

'Patsy must be there and sure that is his daughter there, who died of pneumonia.'

This one time, the whole side of a coffin spilled out at our feet. The skull had detached from the body and looked right at us. You'd think I'd be used to it. But you see by the time the dead get to us, they are packed away nicely in a box. We place the box down safely. Job done. Wait for the next call. Wait for the next death. The next dig. The next grave. We said nothing, only to place the pieces back in and repair the side of the coffin. I grabbed his arm and Tippy held what was left of his leg. Pushed, pushed again. Secured it. Closed it in. Country people don't mind us doing a bit of tidying up while we're down there.

We were mostly in the new cemetery these past few years. Burying young people. Cancer, suicide, farm accidents and drowning are taking the young from our town. The old are living on stubbornly.

I remember the day well. The first day she came. Penelope Mattisa was as beautiful as I'd always imagined an Italian woman to be. She must have a fascination with grave-digging or else she has her eye on one of us. She can have me. I'd turn her on a penny. On the day of a dig, Penelope brought us herbal tea and ham sandwiches. She was off the milk. It didn't agree with her. Tippy threw some whiskey into the blackberry tea, said it made it warmer. Took the nasty taste off it more like. She giggled as she watched us.

'It's lovely to have something warm in my hands on a day like this,' Tippy would be flirting with Penelope. There aren't many of her sorts around these parts so I don't blame him. She had shoulder-length black hair that kicked out at the ends and bobbed as she walked along.

'I like to help. It is a job not easy to do,' she said.

Sometimes she'd bring fig rolls. Chocolate polos too.

If only she knew half the stories we'd heard at wakes. You'd wonder why people would be grieving at all. It's all for show. Happy the person is dead, some of them.

'Do you know what this person died from?' she asked.

The dig was for a young man, who caught some disease in India and came home to recover. He was no sooner recovered when his father stabbed him in the back with the tractor grab. A farm accident. His father didn't know he was there, out getting fresh air.

Penelope held her hand over her mouth and gagged.

'That's the worst I heard,' she said.

'Me too,' I said. 'It's a sad day for his family. His father will never be right after.'

She had yet to bury any of her own. We didn't know much about them. Penelope had settled into the Irish way of things after a bit of a shaky start. I'd heard her husband was a right prick to her, controlling, and made her feel fierce small in company. She left him in Milan; or was it Genoa.

'If you ever die, we'll dig you a fine grave. A nice tidy job,' said Tippy.

'You'll have a long wait. I'm not dying yet.'

Penelope's laugh had cheekiness to it, almost teenage-like. Tippy joined in. It's good to laugh in a graveyard. They looked a right good pair seeing the two of them side by side, bent over laughing at an open grave.

Funerals haven't changed much. The schedule is the same. House. Funeral home. Pub. Church. Cemetery. Hotel. Pub. Then, there's us.

There aren't many around who don't mind getting dirty in the clay that people are rotting in. I don't know what's going to happen to this younger generation. Cremation, I suppose. My father did this before me. He never got paid to do it. It was expected you'd dig for your neighbour or relative and one of theirs would dig for you when your day came. Now, it's different, it's a job that pays. I was already doing the job but had to go for an interview. Imagine. A fella who worked in a bigger graveyard up the North came down for the interview. He had an advanced certificate in grave care. Said he had experience in digging for celebrities and even royalty. I'd tell him where to stick his fucking royalty. Full of shite, he was.

By the time the second interview came round, I had to sit across from suited council men in a hotel room, the John B. Keane suite. I felt like telling them to stick it. They knew I had the chops for the job.

'We were only making sure, Frank,' I was told when I got the call and I accepted their offer.

Graveyards can be the most beautiful of places if people gave them a chance. It is okay to kneel at an altar and talk to someone you've never met. But you're pure daft if you come to a graveyard and talk at the grave of your mother. Let me tell you, an empty graveyard is a damn sad sight.

Kiltrasnack Cemetery is no Glasnevin but we have our so and so's. The first jockey to win the Aintree Grand National is here. A Nobel Prize winner was brought back to be buried in his family plot. Plots closest to him are the most expensive. I'm no salesman so I wouldn't be encouraging it. If I'm being honest, as far away from him as possible is where I'd go. All he did was dis the place.

On the day of a dig, we get on with things. Getting on is key to working in a place like this. I don't stop to think much about the graves of stillborns or children who died from neglect or the teenager who died after a horrific rape ordeal. He used a bottle on her, the court was told. I stop by and say hello to certain ones. I like to stop at the ones I know don't have much family coming to them. You can always tell by the rusted flower pots and the green filth on the angel statues; as thick as seaweed some of it.

The motorbike day, we called it. Well, it was some day. The motorbike headstone was craned in on a watery morning in March. We skipped from side to side, half laughing, half trying to keep warm. It was a work of beauty that headstone. Photos of Jimmy Hoban from different periods in his life were placed across the trunk of the bike. A day in the bog with a turf-dusted sandwich; on to his confirmation day (you can tell by the way his arms were crossed);

fast forward to his wedding photo and a more recent one where he was sitting beside a Stanley range.

'Who'd give Jimmy's bike a good ride? Tippy said as he held on to it by its handlebars. Relatives of Jimmy didn't mind at all. Instead of kneel and pray; they had the words kneel and laugh.

'Ava Gardner would look lovely up there,' said Troy. He was Jimmy's adopted son.

'A motorbike for a headstone, the dead man's wishes,' said Troy. 'He would have enjoyed the fuss, no doubt.'

'Marilyn Monroe for me,' said Tippy.

A local photographer looking to make a few handy quid sent a photo of it to the national press. It made page 3.

It was a dry Sunday afternoon and a lovely day for a dig but I got no call about such business. When the phone rang it was Tippy and he in an awful panic.

'Its Penelope, she's dead.' He said it fast like he didn't want to dwell on the words. They had been on a few dates and Tippy stayed over in Penelope's at weekends. It was getting to the start of the serious phase, that phase where your face and eyes glow at the thought of the person. I'd felt it in myself once so I know it does happen.

'Where are you?'

'I'm on my way to Penelope's. She was stabbed.'

'Is she dead?'

Tippy's voice was breaking.

'Meet me.'

'On the way now,' I said.

I didn't have far to go to get to the cemetery carpark so I knew I'd be there before Tippy. We parked across the road. Men head to toe in white jumpsuits were walking in and out of her house. Special investigation unit was who they were. There was a guard at the entrance to her house, keeping watch. It wasn't long before a crowd trickled down from town.

'A statement will be issued once all of the deceased's family have been notified.' That was all the guards would say.

Tippy only found out after one of the lads in the local told him he'd better get up to Penelope's. 'Swarming with cops up there, bees to honey'.

Tippy wanted to see her.

'Wait, Tippy. Jesus, man, wait. You could be a suspect. They always look at the lover first.'

'I'm not waiting. I want to see her.' I pulled him back as he was about to start into the guard at her gate.

'Now isn't the time.' I pressed down hard on his shoulders and dragged him away towards town. We couldn't say anything to each other. For the next two days, savage rumours went around about her. Running a brothel and harbouring sickos were two that had me thinking this town would take the legs off the parish priest.

Penelope had just had a shower. She was still wet when the killer entered the house. Her body was scraped with a bottle across her legs, abdomen, hands and face. One clean stab to her chest finished the torture.

Tippy didn't know that Francesca, Penelope's sister, was going to be taking her back to Milan.

Tippy didn't know that Penelope hadn't divorced Julio her husband or that she had twin boys, Marco and Lucia. We sat drinking in Darcy's Bar the night of the wake.

'I barely knew her.'

'You knew Penelope, the one who left Italy.'

'I didn't know she had children.'

'They were grown up.'

'She never talked about Italy.'

From Crannóg 40

New Year's Eve
Breid Sibley

after Su-Tung- P'O

The old year is almost gone
slipping away like the sun
over the tree line
of Sleeping Giant Park.
Under the Turner sky
my grandsons play
in snow soft as wool.
The puppy sniffs, digs,
finds grass, is transported,
races circles of delight.
Vivaldi's Winter music
is carried on the air.

Tonight gathered
around the Christmas Tree
my eight year old grandson sleeps.
Eyelashes caressing cheekbones
he rides his puppy above the snow,
while his twelve year old brother
struggles to remain awake.
The sphere is ready to descend
in Times Square, the hum
of thousands like waves on the
seashore.

From Crannóg 31

Night Cycle
Mary Ellen Fean

For the lost children at Tuam

It was another famine, a starvation
of love and mercy –
In this time, a father sets his
daughter on the bar of a bicycle
twenty weeks pregnant and
husbandless, banished from her
people, beyond redemption.

Setting out by night, the next town
is a safe enough distance, a secret to
be kept. An empty road, a fox looks out,
he cannot tell, he feels the heat of her
head against his cheek, as when she was
a little girl, on this same bike.

The nuns would be kind to them, his only
daughter and her child, the winter grazing
on the curate's field is the weight of his
bargain -

Hydrangeas bloom in the convent garden,
cornflower blue, purest white, he sets her
down, his foot on the gravel for balance
her face is a window without a light.

From Crannóg 48

Napoli Abú

Nuala O'Connor

Fuck knows how I ended up going to Naples with a spinster. Not even my spinster but a stray of my sister's, offered up to me as a solution to my singlehood, a partner-in-the-pathetic.

'Beatrice is on her own too,' Clodagh said. 'She's into the kind of stuff you like – you know … art, old ruins, all that. She'd love to go to Italy.'

So we sat side by side – two unbridalled yokes – scrabbling for things to say, though the aeroplane hadn't yet reached 10,000 feet. Beatrice sneezed crazily as the plane climbed.

'Summer cold?' I asked.

'Allergies.'

There's nothing I hate more than the allergy brigade with their I-can't-eat-this and I-can't-tolerate-that and Does-this-have-gluten? Snot-spewed hankies in garlands around them. The only thing worse is a vegan. Jesus wept, I was surely headed into the longest week of my life. I fiddled with my iPod, thinking I could block her out with a consoling waft of Adele, but even I knew that would come off rude. So I tried some conversation.

'Did you read about your man,' I said, 'who fried his wife's placenta and ate it?' Beatrice frowned and I noticed again the colander-shake of freckles across her cheeks, a waste on someone so plain. 'Or the fella who had liposuction and made soap from the fat? Lemon-scented soap. Imagine!'

'I heard a chap on the radio,' she said, 'who cooked his own hip and ate it. He said it tasted of goat.'

'Ah now, that's just mad, isn't it?'

I grinned at her, settled back in my seat and let the aeroplane's thrum wash through me. She mightn't be too bad after all. It could even turn out grand.

Beatrice didn't like Naples. It was too hot altogether, the people stared, the cobbles were too cobbly, the roadworks were over-done and there was way too much graffiti.

'Who, Tara, would deface a thirteenth-century building? Just who?' She put her hand to the graffitied wall as if she might heal it. In Gambrinus she sipped at a caffé latte and wasn't seduced by the pastries, though I would happily have eaten two. After an hour's worth of shopping, I suggested we leave the rush of Via Chiaia to walk the beach; she sloped glumly beside me. 'I hate sand,' she said, sotto voce.

Well, Beatrice, I wanted to say, in that case you can sit on a fucking towel on a bloody fucking bench. But there was something teachery – forceful – about Beatrice and I guessed I would neither swim nor sunbathe that day. Still, I tried.

'I want to go to the beach,' I said, meek as a newt in the face of her scowl.

Beatrice tutted and we trotted on, down towards the water, where even she was mesmerised by the sudden curl of the bay. We stopped to look from one end of the promenade to the other; a squat fort sat to our far left, oddly militaristic in the blur of boats and blue.

'The Bay of Naples. Lovely. I wonder what that is,' I said, indicating the fort.

'It's the Egg Castle. Castell del'Ovo.'

'The Egg Castle? The giant womb, isn't that it? It was probably stuffed full of vestal virgins back in the day. Men, what?'

'You mean prostitutes. Vestals took a vow of chastity.'

I snorted. 'Whatever. Do you think that kept the fellas off them? Men are all the same.'

'No, Tara,' she said, looking at me with those flat eyes, 'they're not.'

We strolled the promenade, though I ached for the lap of seawater on my toes. Before long we stopped at a restaurant for a pee; then we sat on the terrazza to have a drink – she had Orangina. Tee-bloody-total into the bargain, I thought. I started to tell her about Gabriel and, fair play to her, she listened to me banging on about how secretive he is, about the way he keeps everything to himself like some auld Fagin.

'I get fed up badgering for details about his life, so I go silent, but he doesn't seem to notice.' The wine made me tongue-waggy. 'I googled his wife, you know. She's a top-notch solicitor. Super-successful. But square as all get-out, ordinary. Homey. How does she turn Gabriel on? It's a fucking mystery to me. The first rule of shagging married men: never google the wife. Remember that, Beatrice, as you go about your business.'

I sipped my Falanghina and glanced at her: the helmet hair, the miniscule lips, the dour set to her face. Poor shite – what man would look at her?

'My boyfriend is married too,' she said.

'You have a fella?' I sat up and leaned towards her. 'Seriously? A married man? Well, get you, the capaillín dubh.'

'I'm no dark horse, Tara. You expect people to be a certain way, that's all. Because of how they look.'

She needled me with her cloudy eyes and I wasn't sure if she was referring to Gabriel's wife, or to herself. Whatever she meant, it shut me up. I drank my wine and looked out over the sea; the breakers were pearl-tipped and perfect, like waves in a film. The shoreline was spangled with semi-nude bodies, stock-still on towels, soaking up the frazzle.

'Go on, tell me about him,' I said, when she remained silent. 'Did you google the wife?' Beatrice blushed scarlet. 'You did, you mad thing!'

'I didn't need to; I know his wife.'

'Tut-tut, naughty-naughty, Beatrice, crapping on your own doorstep. That's worse than what I'm at – at least Gabriel is a work thing.'

'How is it worse or better or anything, Tara? We can care about it or not care about it, as we choose. I don't see that what I'm doing is good, bad or indifferent compared to your situation.'

'So who is he? Who is she?'

Beatrice tossed her head forward and pulled a bandanna over her hair; she tied it at the nape of her neck. She wouldn't look at me.

'I'd rather not say,' she said eventually.

'Do I know him?'

She glanced at me, uneasy but cocky. 'You do.'

'It's not Phelim is it?' I snorted at the idea of anyone having an affair with my tub-tastic brother in law, but Beatrice had turned forty shades of puce. 'Jesus Christ on a bike! Listen, you're welcome to him.' I thought of Clodagh suffering Phelim all these years and here was the bugger having an affair. With Beatrice, of all people. I tipped the rest of the wine down my neck. 'Will we walk up to the castle?' I said.

'Sure.'

Castell del'Ovo was long and flat-topped, punched with tiny windows; it sat in the sea on an island, as if it had risen from the water and anchored itself there.

'It doesn't look like an egg,' I said.

'It's not supposed to. They say Virgil put a magical egg into the foundations to hold the place up. If the shell got broken, the castle would collapse and Naples along with it.'

'Can you go in and look at the egg?'

Beatrice reared her head back and gawped at me and, for the first time, she laughed. And she didn't just laugh, she nearly puked up her Orangina she was gasping so much to catch her breath between guffaws. After each spasm she waved her hand and thumped her craw; she would look up at me for a second and burst again into hoots.

'For fuck's sake, Tara,' she said, between groans as her laughter died down. 'Oh my Lord.'

'What?' I said.

'God, Tara, you're gas. Did you not hear when I said the egg was magic? Bewitched!'

She giggled and set herself off into gales again. I like when people laugh – I'm a good-humoured kind of person and even though I

knew she was laughing at me, the mad sound of her was infectious and I was soon chortling too. We stood on the prom, a pair of Hiberno hyenas, barely able to stand for the gusts of laughter breaking through us. When we finally calmed ourselves, I linked Beatrice's arm and we sauntered on towards the castle.

'Ah, it's all crazy, isn't it, Bea?' I said.

'It is.'

'Men. Love. The whole shebang. You know, I keep getting spam that says things like "Marriage is boring, affairs are fun". It's like the universe knows what I'm at and wants to annoy me.'

'But if it's not fun, why do you bother?' Beatrice said.

'I never said it wasn't fun.'

'You're threatened by his wife's job. Is that fun?'

I turned to her. 'Are you threatened, now that I know you're trying to steal my sister's husband?'

'Steal him?' Beatrice laughed. 'What on earth would I do with him, Tara? I don't want to own Phelim.'

'No, I suppose not,' I said. 'Meanwhile I have no clue why I picked Gabriel to love, the most reticent man on the planet. But, there you go – I can't even do affairs right.'

'You love this Gabriel?'

'Ah, I suppose I do. Until the next one comes along.'

She broke away from me and turned to descend some steps that lead to the beach; I followed her. I took off my sandals; the sand was talc soft and hot under my soles. Beatrice kicked off her runners. We walked to the water's edge and let lacy waves wash over our feet.

'The first person we fall in love with shapes us, don't they?' Beatrice said.

'Is Phelim the only man you've ever loved?'

Beatrice shrugged. 'That first one moulds our idea of love, I think.'

'I bloody well hope not. My first was a self-focussed manipulator. A redhead. Turned me off redsers forever.'

Beatrice pulled one foot through the water, watched its lazy arc. 'Do you ever think about family?' she said. 'Kids?'

'Brats? Gabriel says he'll give me a baby if I really want one. I'm hurtling towards forty. Not sure I need all that now.' I looked at her; the reflection of the Mediterranean made a beatific glow of her face. She smiled – one of those involuntary ones that slip up onto the lips because they can't be held down, a smile that's married to a secret. 'Come here, Beatrice, you're not pregnant are you?' A flash of childless Clodagh lit up my inner eye.

'No, no. Not at all,' she said.

Her eyes were trained on the Castell del'Ovo and she stared at that place as if all she knew or cared about would burst up from under its foundations and lay itself on the shifting waves before her, like some sort of answer to everything. Or maybe she expected an egg to rise up; a magical egg that could burrow deep inside and alter a life.

From Crannóg 40

Potsdamer Platz, Sometime
John Walsh

Gisela asks me to make the ride with her.
It's a nightmare alone.
There's a guy in Berlin. She ends up
marrying him, but not for long.

It is a ride into the landscape of nihilism,
the mindset of verboten,
the pulse of virtual transit.
No matter what happens, don't stop,
Gisela warns me as the headlights rail
against the night. The Wall is an afterthought,
a cryptic reminder of where it is not at.

They wait two months after I leave, then knock it.
These days I make breaches of my own,
hammer and chisel tempo, close to the bone.
Potsdamer Platz. Don't stop! Gisela tells me.
I'm on the right track. She's been there.
Sometimes the end is in undoing the done.

From Crannóg 18

Reunion at Ceannt Station
Rachel Coventry

Just this, no pain, no clawing elation
till sparks relight the touch and I flare,
sit quiet in the cool of the station.

Be grateful for this sudden privation
alone with the birds and the birds don't care,
just this, no pain, no clawing elation.

Do not swear any hot invocation
let the sloshing of this tide drain away
sit quiet in the cool of the station.

Some woman aging, someone's relation,
not who you were but who you are today
just this, no pain, no clawing elation.

You, the darkness, and the frustration
the anger in you, its final decay
sit quiet in the cool of the station.

Finally to greet emancipation,
I am only this and it's only fair
just this, no pain no clawing elation
sit quiet in the cool of the station.

From Crannóg 37

25

Rising
Vinny Steed

I
am the ears of a sugar plant
strained, hearsay of leaves
earth-arrhythmia
I am the tiller of dreams.

I
am a foreign language
grounded, small syllables forged
in darkness, root-rumblings
a secret softly woken.

I
am the gutter-seed
emboldened, nestled on the back
of larvae, root and giant
grub. I am star-searching.

I
am sapling
opened, shooting for words
born of clay and air
I am stalk-stuttering.

I
am tree-bearing
rising pool of noise, vocal fibres deep
Listen to the roar of my stomata
Branches chattering with the gods.

From Crannóg 47

She Walks
Bernie Crawford

She walks because the men with guns could rape her
She walks because her mother told her to

She walks because the men with bombs will kill her
She walks to keep up with the others

She walks because the dark shadows under her bed
now live in every room of her home

She walks because her school is a heap of stones
with pieces of porcelain ink wells sparkling among them

She walks because the stall where she bought
falafels in pitta pockets is gone

She walks because the tattered sneakers of the boy,
who sold spices in newspaper cones, lie among the rubble of
the market

She walks because it is easier to walk than to stop
She walks because she is a child

She walks to find the piece that flew from her heart,
out through her mouth, the day the air strikes started

She walks to forget the piece that flew from her heart
that day the air strikes started

She walks

From Crannóg 43

The Workhouse
Claire Loader

It was Michael who died first. He was born from the weakness of my mother, frail, like a lonely tree windswept on the bog. You could see in her eyes, day after day, sorrow and pure exhaustion vying and pulling behind her dead, listless stare. Daddy didn't have the strength to bury him proper. Whisked by a fox from a shallow grave, our only comfort was that at least something had eaten that night.

It wasn't long before sickness came and took Colm too. He'd been the strongest of us all but it didn't seem to matter. I would often sit out alone on the path, twisting and turning the tatters of my skirt as the soft hues of day's end melted into twilight. The wagtail, so jolly at my feet, would head back to his nest and leave me with the stars, as one by one they crept out from the blanket of the sky, almost winking just at me.

I imagined them all to be angels, but it was hard to believe they could bear watching us all fall one by one. Watch as the fields lay fallow and the light of each cottage was snuffed out forever. There weren't many of us left now, the path quiet as I slowly slinked back home, the hard pads of my feet scuffing the dirt as I trudged up to the door. I knew it wouldn't be long now, the few scraps of dignity my parents had left were wearing thin. It was nearly time.

We weren't alone the day we finally conceded and made our way towards the village, our meagre possessions feeling heavy in our pockets. We were joined by more defeated souls on the slow march up the boreen, slipping out of the thicket like ghosts. No one said a word as we all slowly swayed up the track, like sheer blades of grass being softly blown from side to side, with so little as a wisp of skin keeping us from being lifted away.

We passed the walls of the grand house along the way, just able to spy the tall tower peeking out at us from above the surround. I'd never had a chance to go in; some I knew who served there, a lucky few not bound to the whims of nature, the blights and the scourges. I wondered, looking up at the tower, how the sky could still be so blue.

I'd only heard stories of the workhouse, my parents whispering at night in the light of the dying embers, whispering in fevered tones, hints of fear reaching me as I snuggled deeper into the blanket, trying desperately to forget the emptiness that gnawed inside my belly. It almost didn't register now, it was simply a new constant, one that held me close as we finally reached the main entrance and stood wavering at the gates.

They separated us when we eventually went in. Mammy didn't even cry as they led the men through a door to the right, and us off to the left. I never did see Dad again, his slow lanky figure my last memory as he shuffled through the door. They put all the women in the back block, the mess hall separating the men's yard from ours, dinner timed so we would never meet.

The younger children were sent to a separate block, away from the adults. The windows so high looking out onto the yard, that their mothers couldn't reach to see out. Although some still tried, desperately trying to hoist each other up on weak arms, just to catch a glimpse.

The nights were filled with moaning, broken only by a whimper, a cough. Mammy stopped talking altogether and it wasn't long until she just lay in the sleeping quarters, unable to go down to work in the laundry, just waiting to die. They buried her out in the field to the side of our block, a mound among many, a small pile of dirt pushing out from beneath the dandelions.

Life became a game of miserable repetition, filled with smells and sickness and death. I thought about the wagtail sometimes, mostly in the evening light, and wondered if he was still out in the meadow somewhere, flitting amongst the trees. I wondered if I would ever get out of here, or if I too was destined for the little field, where I could finally lie down and comfort my mother.

I slowed down the car, trying to peer inside the gap in the gate.

'Hey, what's that place, I wonder?'

'I dunno, it's not coming up on the GPS – do you wanna take a look?'

'Fuck it sure, why not?'

We pulled into the side of the road and parked in front of a small field. Several small rocks stuck out of the long grass, faint etchings indecipherable on their smooth, weather beaten surface. The rusty chain on the gate creaked and groaned as we edged the sides open and slid under the stone arch. A long, tall grey building ran down the left to meet the paddock below. Boarded-up windows and thick streams of ivy told of a structure long out of use.

We found an old side door down the far end, that sprinkled the ground with splinters and dust as we shoved and broke the rotting wood. Through a low tunnel, we emerged into a large square courtyard, enclosed on each side by a single-storey building to the right and a high wall to the left. A tall, four-storey building sat at the back, the wind whipping noisily through the missing tiles of the roof, like an old, tired orchestra. We jumped, trying to peer in through the windows, gaining flashes of broken wood, perhaps a table.

'Jesus, what was this place, do ya reckon? It's huge.'

'A school, I wonder? Maybe a factory?'

Our shoes sent up small showers of stones as we crunched our way over the yard, setting the crows to flight. They circled, cawing and cackling above the empty hollow buildings, their cries, like children screeching and playing, bounced off the walls to surround us in constant echo.

A movement to my right set my head to turn as a crow landed near my foot, cocking its beak in a curious stare before taking flight once more.

I watched it heave its wings and fly over the wall into the field beyond, the thicket of tall grass and dandelions engulfing it from below. The courtyard suddenly felt cold; the dark, empty windows stared down at us, menacing. The wind picked up and, shivering, I hugged my jacket closer to my chest.

'Hey, you wanna get outa here? It's getting cold and this place is kinda creepy.'

'Ya, we should go. I'm getting hungry.'

From Crannóg 47

On Oranienburger Strasse
Deirdre Kearney

The whores are out in force tonight.

On this street where the ghost children play
sleek beauties ply their trade
in thigh-high boots and skimpy tops.

When recession bites, it's tough.
So many give it away for nothing now.

By pavement cafés
glassy dead eyes cajole
and plead.

As I catch her eye
in that one brief moment
she sees her mother.

From Crannóg 32

Now That You Are Gone
Ria Collins

In memory of my mother

The crows in the belfry croak their chilled call,
the clouds above shudder with cold.

I left you looking for me across stars at night,
throwing holy water that fell to the ground

while I rode camels through the desert
escaping the parched boredom

like a balloonist
distant and removed, in motion.

My letters neatly ordered in a drawer,
I trace unguent Vicks and pills and half used face cream,

touch worn rosary-beads and medals,
hair strands in your comb,

pink lipstick almost used,
lace handkerchief in a drooping pocket

of your worn and faded gown
perfumed with lavender,

the new one I gave you neatly folded
amongst the unused thermal vests.

Torn out pages of recipes
spill like bruised memories across a blue pain,

sometimes I pretend you are still here
labelling warm marmalade jars in the kitchen.

The younger you full of laughter
chasing us out to school after breakfast

of porridge and Clonakilty black pudding,
is a faded make-believe in ochre.

Yes you pushed your self-righteous
exhausted torrent of despair on us,

when I travelled the distance to visit,
five days invariably became two,

but I miss you like an amputated limb
that burns and stings with real imaginings.

The bell peals for Mass and the rooks take flight,
rain pours, I hide in your room ; unseen.

It will pass as all things, leaving only
its scent behind, a lingering trace of having been.

From Crannóg 51

Pigeon of Patience
Christine Valters Paintner

Each morning
you perch
outside my window,
look out over
the lake of rooftops
wait, puff, coo,
for me to feed you.

Some days I forget,
or rush on, I don't even
like the grey feathers
coated with city grime,
tiny orange eyes, head bobs,
instead I wish for
starlings and sparrows,

but still you return
sometimes with friends,
reminding me of what it is
to hunger and hope
and still I scatter seeds.

From Crannóg 49

Sticks of Pomegranate
Betsey Carreyette

If I could take these sticks
from the raised hands of donkey driving boys
hold them high above the clattering carts

I could meld
into the evening shade
sipping tea from tiny cups.
I wouldn't have to stir;

If I could slip these entwined
pomegranate sticks
beneath
this slipping ball of flame,

scoop –
its dissolving mass from the fractured sky,

the call to Ishaa would never come

nor, the Matruh bus
outside El Sulieman draw.

*El Sulieman Mosque- the point from which the mini bus
leaves for Marsa Matruh after Ishaa prayer, the final
prayer of the day, performed after sunset.*

From Crannóg 31

The Autumn Evenings are Closing In
Sue Fahy

She has for a watchdog
the magpie that chatters
volubly and long
when twilight falls.

Yes, she notices
there is only one
the one for sorrow
she accepts her sorrow

and does not rise
at the behest of a cry
to peer for a shape
or even a shadow;

her husband, perhaps
coming in from the meadow
the rake's wooden handle
slung over his shoulder.

From Crannóg 40

The Innocent Cosmopolitan
Emily Cullen

If I imagine I'm Dorothy Parker
expel smoke slowly from a cigarette holder
in a silken kimono on a languid afternoon,
conjure my wit while pounding keys,
a brandy and lime within easy reach.

If I feign I am Lauren Bacall,
unamused by the jejune, gesture
through an alluring smokescreen,
arch a piqued brow as I smoulder
demurely at Humphrey Bogart.

If I channel Coco Chanel,
loll in shimmering sweeps of pearls,
behind a fanlike spray of fronds
will I get beyond girlish feelings
to that swagger I secretly long for?

Am I palsied by the claim
I'm 'innocently cosmopolitan',
the taunt of an old flame?
Fine, if one can fairly say, I'll be
at the apogee of suavity one day.

From Crannóg 49

First Tuesdays

Evelyn Parsons

Spluttering smoke, their blue Corolla turns left at the gate, rounds the bend at Duffy's house, disappearing past their washing line. Pegged sheets flap, waving their Mam and Dad good riddance.

As soon as they're out of sight, Leanne dashes to the backdoor. She's small for her age and though Shannon's older, *she's* even smaller. Smallness runs in the family, their Mam keeps saying, - makes them prone.

On tiptoes, Leanne stretches fingertips to the rusty bolt, saws it back and forth, back and forth. It gives too quickly in the end clipping her finger. Eyes watering, Leanne sucks the pain, flings open the door with her good hand and there's Shannon. Her t-shirt's drenched, plastered to a chest ridged like potato drills this time of year, deep and straight and empty.

Half hidden through a rain-frizzled fringe, Shannon's black eyes study her reaction like a mirror. Leanne's careful to show nothing. Not a flicker. She gives Shannon the smile, pulling stray wisps of hay from her dripping hair. Besides, Shannon's reasonable, considering. Thanks to suffering Christ, Leanne thinks, not God. God's not around here much.

'Would you come in, come in, come in, why don't you, Ms Fleming and warm yourself in front of the fire?' Leanne says, copying the voice Mam uses with 'that shower.'

If she hears her, Shannon's not smiling. Shannon half falls, half trips over the splintered lintel, her toe catching in torn lino. Leanne links her past the paint bubbling walls of the back hall, shivering, to the kitchen. She feels smaller than before. Of the three of them, Shannon has it worse. The bad attitude. She smells of dry hay and wet dog and sure enough Dog slopes in behind her, shaking his matted coat.

Drops spray Tommy but Tommy doesn't cry. He stops crawling, sits still, uncertain, green snot bubbling his nostrils, staring up at Shannon's new face.

'I've just got the kettle on and dinner's in the oven Ms Fleming.' Leanne says, copying the drawn out way their Mam says Mizzzzzzzz, like the static humming of a badly tuned radio or a manic bluebottle frantic to escape. It's normally worth a smile.

'Will it be tea or coffee today?' Leanne throws a dry blanket around her.

'Mizzzzzzzzzz Fleming?' Leanne persists before getting her reward. The gap in her smile makes people think Shannon's younger than thirteen.

When Shannon remembers the game she swallows the smile, tries to look serious, putting her head to one side like Ms Fleming does. She does a brilliant Ms Fleming.

'Coffee if it's handy Mrs. Casey,' Shannon says.

She sits down beside the unlit fireplace, hands out to warm them just like Ms Fleming does. Tommy crawls towards the cold ashes before Leanne snatches him to put him building towers with cans.

'Careful you don't catch fire there now,' Leanne says. 'Milk and sugar?'

'Ah not at all, you'll need the milk for the children when they come in from school,' says Shannon.

'Go on, go on, go on, Ms Fleming,' Leanne says, 'sure we have plenty. It's throwing it away I am.'

Leanne gets a dirty mug from the sink, rinses it, filling it to the top from the tap.

'Mind you don't burn yourself Ms Fleming'. Leanne hands it to Shannon, cracked side furthest from her burst lip.

'That's funny looking coffee if you don't mind me saying, Mrs. Casey,' Shannon says, gulping it down.

Leanne peers into the mug in Shannon's hand.

'Jesus, you're right Ms Fleming. It's water, that's why. It's always happening round here. It's unbelievable the amount of times Paddy and I buy milk and coffee and its water they give us, that crowd of inbreds down in Spar. But sure they couldn't be right, could they Ms Fleming, and the type of families they come from?'

'But now what will your poor children do for milk when they come from school for the dinner?'

'Ah, but sure it's not milk at all they take with the dinner.'

'Not milk, Mrs. Casey?'

'No Ms Fleming. Not milk.

'But what then? Water?'

'Ah not at all, 'Leanne says, 'It's wine!'

'Wine Mrs. Casey? The children? With their dinner?' Shannon giggles leaving down the empty mug to pull Tommy onto her knee. He's nearly as big as her already.

'Fussy eaters Ms Fleming. And that's the only way they'll have it. Wine with chicken nuggets and beer with sausages.'

'Beer with sausages Mrs. Casey?'

'That's right Ms Fleming. Only the best for my children. I'm a great believer in the importance of a good diet. Could you make a note of that Ms Fleming?'

Shannon points her index finger and writes with it on Tommy's back. He wriggles, liking the tickle, and leans back against Shannon.

'Oh and don't forget Ms Fleming, write down as well – they like brandy with bacon. They'll have nothing but brandy to bring out the flavor. And as you know, I always serve them what they like.'

'Sure you're the best mother in Ireland Mrs. Casey!'

The girl's look at each other, gasp, momentarily half shocked, then peal with laughter, great whooping yelps. Shannon's ribs move in and out like an accordion, so skinny they 're jabbing Tommy. He slides off her lap. Leanne's barely able to draw breaths. Dog's tail wags like he got the joke too, a dull thumping applause against the lino. After a moment even Tommy smiles.

Shannon's cut reopens .Her lip starts bleeding again, not much, but enough to bring her down. She stops, goes silent. Tommy stares at Shannon, his pale face serious. Her eyes fill up and her chin wobbles so Leanne says quickly,

'Oh, we're having bacon today Ms Fleming.'

Shannon makes no response.

'Oh you don't believe me, is that it?' Leanne tries again. 'Well would you like to look in the oven so?'

She reaches up, opens the oven. A lump of cold grease with moldy green fur rests in the roasting pan. A dried up chip curls in on itself. Just for a second she marvels at how it got left over.

'Mmmmmm ... 'Leanne says, 'Smell that . See.' She stands back.

Shannon straightens up and looks in. The smell of stale grease is gross.

'Mmmmmmm ... Lovely, Mrs. Casey but ... I can't see any bacon.' She shakes her head and points her fingerpen to take another note. 'No. No bacon here Mrs. Casey.'

Leanne does their Mam's shocked face, the wide eyed starey one with the mouth hanging open like she's been robbed.

'Are you making a liar of me Ms Fleming? ' Leanne puts her hands on her hips, raises her chin in the air. 'Look in, I tell you.'

Shannon stretches higher and leans in again. 'No, Mrs. Casey, definitely no bacon... only now I can see a roast chicken, no, two roast chickens or is it three?' She's giggling again. 'And gravy and potatoes and ice cream and stuffing and beans and Chef's tomato sauce.' Shannon's favorites, all of them. Legs like sticks poke from under her t-shirt.

'I'll certainly have to make a note of that. Well aren't you a great cook entirely Mrs. Casey, bacon or no bacon.'

'I am indeed,' Leanne says, 'and do you know

what else? Didn't I forget, today's the first Tuesday. Isn't Paddy gone to town with the child benefit to do the shopping and he'll be bringing home the bacon too.'

'Are you sure it wasn't his car I passed parked below at the Lock Inn this morning, Mrs. Casey?'

'Ah not at all Ms Fleming.' Leanne roars, struggling to remain serious. 'What would *he* be doing in the Lock Inn? Sure my Paddy doesn't drink!'

The girls can't hold back uproarious laughter. Tommy looks up from stacking a tower of Carlsberg and smiles at his sisters, happy once more.

'Will you make a note of that Ms Fleming?' Leanne says when she gets her breath back.

'I ... will ... if I can ... stop ... laughing ... but,' Shannon squeals, struggling to keep the social worker's persona going , 'I'm sure ... it was ... his Corolla ... with the big dent in it from the time ... the gate was ... in the wrong place.'

'It couldn't be Ms Fleming. Isn't he driving a Ferrari now? And anyway my Paddy's gone to work.'

'Work? With his bad back?' Shannon creases again hands holding her tummy. 'Is it in the Lock Inn Mrs. Casey?'

'Not at all. Work in ...'. Leanne thinks of the place teacher talked about the last day she got to school. The place furthest away. 'In Australia Ms Fleming.

And ... and he doesn't even need a back to be ....' She's thinking hard ... 'singing,' she says at last.

'Singing?'

'That's right.'

'The Fields of Athenry, is it? Our lullaby? The same half verse over and over?' Shannon continues. 'In Australia? And he'll be back soon with the bacon?'

Tommy freezes and looks towards the door. Their mirth dies. In silence the girls look at each other.

'He will,' Leanne says slowly at last, 'and I'm going to kill him with this when he does, Ms Fleming. Could you make a note of that?'

Leanne picks up the frying pan and waves it wildly in the air. Shannon's hand flies to her eye and she cowers. The dog whimpers. Tommy starts crying. Leanne leaves it down quickly.

'Jesus I'm sorry. Shush shush Tommy.' She picks him up, jiggles him a bit, he buries his snuffling nose in her top. Tommy doesn't cry much. 'It's alright, it's alright, and it's only me Tommy. Leanne. Only playing.

Shannon keeps her hands on her head, her scrawny wrists covered in bruises. She's always been the most prone. Her legs are like a bird's. Their Dad says she gets the finest of scraps out of the goodness of his heart. They know those scraps, so does Dog. The goodness of Dad's heart's another matter. Shannon's eyes are massive in her face, even with the swelling reducing them to slits.

'Don't worry. It's the first Tuesday.' Leanne says.' They won't be back until the Lock throws them out or the money is gone and either way they won't be fit to lift a finger to us.

The fridge is empty apart from tonic water and an empty juice carton. Leanne climbs a chair to open the press. There are a few cornflakes, tins that aren't much use without an opener, and a heel of bread growing green freckles. Leanne roots around the back of the cupboard, finds two sausages wrapped in newspaper hidden from last night's dinner.

'Here, we can heat these in the toaster.'

Shannon pays no attention. Instead she opens the window to release a trapped moth fluttering feebly against the dirty pane.

Smells of turf smoke drift in from Duffy's. It's after three. The Duffy kids are home from school, playing outside and laughing, screeching, kicking ball. Their house is two fields, a ditch and a line of trees away but it might as well be a million miles. Mrs. Duffy's calling them in. Their dinner's ready.

The rain has stopped, the sky's all cried out. It doesn't much matter what the weather does tonight. On first Tuesdays everyone sleeps inside the snoring house.

From Crannóg 29

Signs

Tom Lavelle

After aunt Rose came back,
my mother took Dad
up to Tesco,
showed him where
they stack the baskets,
steered him up and down
the aisles, pointing out
the bits and pieces he'd need.
She roped my brother in
to drive her down to Limerick,
to call on Mary, her bridesmaid,
who'd been poorly for some time.
Headed off to Fairymount,
to throw her eye over
the hilly acres her mother hailed from,
then north to Donegal,
to linger outside her childhood home,
her mind running down
the wet Lifford streets.
She took her children by surprise
with presents and remarks
that seemed off-beat at the time.

After aunt Rose came back,
smiling in a dream and said,
'We're waiting.'

From Crannóg 30

Somewhere in Picardy

Stephen de Búrca

There was no breeze
the time we walked away
from the desolate village.
Where the slope levelled,
            nothing was beyond
our sight of corn-fields.

On a patch of grass
by the road, we stopped
to consider the poppies.
We must come earlier
            next year, you said:
their red had begun to fade

but enough was left for us
to sit there and share a
thermos of lukewarm coffee.
Christ, how I can
            recall
that metallic drop –

the wire-thin copper ring,
always loose on your little finger
against the thermos, a foreign
sound so necessary for us to be
            folded upon.

Perhaps the poppies still are there.
Surely, they will have been
            and been again.

From Crannóg 50

33

The Ballad of Cross-Eyed Kate
Jarlath Fahy

(To the air of Di Provenza il mar from Verdi's La Traviata)

How long have I loved thee cross-eyed kate
As long as your prosthetic leg is put on straight
And your washed-out wig is at its proper angle
That arm you lost in last year's mangle
Down all the years dilapidations
Through arthritis haemorrhoids and ulcerations
After all the pain of reconstruction
I love your botox and liposuctions
I don't mind that your breath is laboured
If it wasn't cheese and onion flavoured

It's true you never stayed at home
You were always inclined to roam
Paragliding was your obsession
Between the elations and depressions
Until like Icarus you crashed into a tree
Losing your leg up to the knee
Things were never the same as they were before
As you crawled along the floor

Now every morning after eight
I set you upright on your skates
And I push with all my might
As you skate off into the light
Twenty years went by so sweet
Then you lost your buckteeth
Swinging from a trapeze
They replaced both your knees
when your hair went on fire
you got enmeshed in wire
after the oil tank exploded
driving round a bend blindfolded

From Crannóg 44

The European Knitting Club
Mary O'Rourke

We came from Galway, Lille, Munich, Barcelona
Some experts, more beginners.
Around a blazing fire
We discussed stitches
Scarves, jumpers, socks
Skeins of wool, balls of wool,
A kaleidoscope of colour
Patterns, small needles, big needles
Crochet hooks of all sizes

Hot chocolate was welcome
As we exchanged ideas;
An impromptu language class began
Eager to gain fluency
The foreigners picked up words
Dropped stitches
Started all over again
As they spoke about the past in the present tense
Discussed dialects and idioms
And strained their ears to understand

The only tension was in the wool;
Our common threads
English and knitting

From Crannóg 31

The Ballad of Tullykyne

Nicola Geddes

King is to castle as tower is to rook
My sister's fort is as tall as mine
The rain it battered and the wind it shook
She watches me from behind her line
Her eyes hard and wary, she stares out alone
Cold creeping into each cranny and nook
She thinks she is safe in her fortress of stone
King is to castle as tower is to rook

High is the tower and cold is the brook
At a table for one she is served up her wine
The cup to her lips like an old fish hook
On touching her tongue the drink sours to brine
And cursing and spitting she clutches her throne
Her face is reset in that pinched, crooked look
As old and as cracked as the grey limestone
King is to castle as tower is to rook

My sister the witch! My sister the crook!
I call up her ruin, and wait for the sign
I cast down three stones and forward I look
To the fall of the fortress of old Tullykyne
But the storm that crashed down, and the wind that was blown
The strength of the lightning, oh how I mistook!
The cry of defeat was both hers and my own
King is to castle as tower is to rook

Raven and crow, jackdaw and rook
A young man came by in black feathers so fine
In his right hand a knife, in his left was a book
He fashioned figures from my sister's spine

A miniature horse from my collarbone
He wound our hair round his button hook
Before setting the pieces on the square cornerstone
King is to castle as tower is to rook

Our deeds are forgotten, our names are unknown
The crows all gather on the ruin by the brook
The gorse, the fuchsia and the hawthorn have grown
King is to castle as tower is to rook.

From Crannóg 45

Mother May I

Ger Burke

I get out of the car, walk towards the parking meter and tug at the long scarf I'd wound like a noose around my neck. A gobful of chewing gum plastered on the edge of the money slot nauseates me. As I rummage in my bag for my purse, I'm careful to avoid the pink mass. I insert two euro and five twenty-cent coins before struggling back to the car to rest my weight against the bonnet, feeling faint. My stomach clenches and I vomit the porridge I ate for breakfast. Unwinding my scarf, I open my windcheater and sit into the car leaving the door open.

Two teenagers stare at the ground. 'Ugh, gross,' one remarks. 'And she must be forty.'

'Yeah. If we puked like that, they'd say we'd been on the beer and have us locked up.'

They lift the last syllable of the final word an octave higher but I'm used to how young people talk; my students speak in exactly the same way. At least they did the last time the medics considered me well enough to teach.

Apparently my problems stem from my childhood, but no time to fixate on that now. Need to reach the pharmacy for my repeat prescription. I stick the ticket to the windscreen, lock the car and set off in the direction of the city centre.

As I walk across the car park to the Salmon Weir Bridge, I obsess about a children's game I used to play called *Mother May I?* I hear again the 'mother' announce a direction. 'Joan you may take three giant steps forward.'

'Mother may I?'

'You may not.'

Sometimes I'd be so jittery I'd forget to ask and would be sent back to the starting line. I'd never been the one to touch 'mother' first.

When I come onto the crowded main street, my legs turn to jelly. Two men are leaning over the bridge looking into the river but, thankfully, they are too absorbed to notice me when I stop beside them to rest. After a few minutes I move on. Taking 'baby steps,' I sidle by their protruding rear ends, head down. I must take 'giant steps.' The sooner I collect my medication, the sooner I'll get home to Mother; she'd been dozing on a chair asleep when I'd left her.

There are too many people on Eglinton Street. My palms start to sweat and I feel my heart racing. I escape into a church, stand in the entrance and breathe deeply.

I'd love to stay and enjoy the stillness, but I must hurry. Even though I left a note for the home help to tell her where I'm gone, Mother will be upset if I'm not there when she wakes up.

As I leave the church, I pass a man with a baby strapped in front. I have to resist an impulse to wipe away the dribbles that fall from the teething brat. I imagine the baby looks like my brother.

I always maintain that I'm an only child. But there were two of us. My brother was born when I was five so I was old enough to notice when Mother's stomach stretched and her belly button turned inside out like a mushroom stalk. Old enough to remember touching it, she flinching, her reprimand.' What on earth did you do that for?'

Most afternoons my mother went upstairs to the bedroom and lay down. 'I want you to be quiet, Joan,' she'd say. 'You're not to bother me unless the house is on fire.' Once when I didn't heed her, she locked me in the press until she got up. Her attitude towards me during her pregnancy changed. She became distant and preoccupied.

I'm still unclear whether, at first, my mother wanted the baby or not but I hated the idea of an intruder. She was *my* mother. Father was away a lot from that time on so I figure he wasn't too keen on the idea either.

It was near Christmas when the baby was born and of course they christened him Noel. It bothered me a lot for the first few days. Then my aunt spoiled me and gave me lots of sweets and after a while I was able to forget him. He wasn't in my face all the time then.

But when my mother came home, it seemed to me that Noel was stuck to her. 'Isn't he beautiful Joan? So handsome,' she used to enthuse.

Any time I wanted a cuddle, he was there, like glue. 'You should give him a smack,' I advised her once before going to bed. 'He never shuts up.' I spent a lot of time that night desolate and angry, listening to him cry.

Next morning when I went in to see him, he was silent. His face was pressed into the mattress, his skin a light shade of blue. When I put my arm through the cot bar, I felt him stiff and cold.

I remember closing the door behind me, creeping back into my bed, pulling the sheets over my head and lying in the dark, feeling sick. I thought I had been quiet but I must have woken Mother. A few minutes later, I heard her feet dragging across the landing to the bathroom and then to Noel's room. Seconds later she screamed.

The honking of a car horn brings me back. Shaking my head, I rid myself of memories and look at my watch. One o'clock. It's been so long since I've collected the medication myself, I'm unsure if the pharmacy closes for lunch or not. I'd have forgotten where it was except that I know it's next door to a florist.

My stomach rumbles, reminding me that I've emptied its contents onto the car park. I have no appetite but I hear Mother's voice, in my head, forceful, as it had been before her illness, ordering me to eat and 'keep my strength up.' I'm torn between 'obeying' and hurrying. I do what I usually do, acquiesce.

Overcoming my distaste for fast food, I enter a takeaway. 'Hamburger and French fries please,' I say.

'Medium or large? Drink?'

As often as possible, I think. Now that I seldom meet my teaching colleagues and Mother confiscates any alcohol she sees, It's ages since I had a gin-and-tonic.

I pay for the food and wait, observing the other customers. A girl with scarlet lips pushes aside her empty carton of chips and chicken wings. 'Bloody piece of chicken stuck in my tooth,' she complains to her companion as she pokes with her index finger deep into her mouth. 'Got it.' At a table next to the door, a man lounges in his chair his glance fixed on the street; his mouth opens in a yawn. A child in a red dress toddles by the counter holding a doll by its leg. She retrieves her fat soother from the floor, smiles at me and wraps her lips around it. My stomach heaves. Thoughts of sinking my teeth into an oily hamburger make me feel worse. I leave the counter and stumble towards the door, my feet feeling like lead weights.

The sounds of percussion instruments swell from a music shop, soft melodies from a beauty parlour, ballads, loud and off-key, from a busker. This cacophony mingles with the purr of cars and the rattle of a bus pulling away from a stop. I'd love to scream.

Realising I need my medicine badly, I walk faster. Nobody moves out of my way. I 'd like to kill the man who continues to walk straight at me, but instead I heave a deep breath and step off the kerb to weave my way between the edge of the path and the oncoming traffic.

As I approach the pharmacy, men wearing hard hats pound the tarmac with pneumatic drills. From somewhere, as if from hell, Johnny Cash sings, 'I fell into a burning ring of fire.'

Mother is emphatic that when she dies she wants her body burned; she detests the idea of worms wriggling into her mouth and feeding on her stomach.

Losing track of where I'm going, I crash into an overflowing rubbish bin. 'Sorry, sorry, I'm really sorry,' I say.

A woman stares in amazement. 'What the hell's wrong with her?'

I round the corner and push open the door of the pharmacy next to the florist. 'At last,' I whisper. The carpet is springy under my runners. I breathe the perfumed air with relief. 'Joan Casby.' I speak slowly, conscious of how acute anxiety makes me sound incoherent. 'I've come to renew my prescription.'

A woman emerges from behind the counter and says to the assistant, 'I'll deal with this, Mary.'

'Ok, Gran.'

There is concern in the older woman's eyes. I think of Mother this morning, lying slumped in a chair, her head sideways, her mouth open, the radio blaring beside her. Maybe I should have woken her before I left, but she's bad tempered when I discover her catnapping; I need my tablets before I can cope with one of her moods. The woman leads me to the back of the shop and opens the door to a small room. 'In here. No one will bother us.' Her brow is furrowed, her tone sympathetic.

'Sit down Joan.' She gestures to a chair and I sit, perched on the edge, leaning forward.

She stands with her back to a radiator. 'I don't know what to say.' She swallows. 'Excuse me, but I'm finding this difficult.'

I wait while she composes herself, my palms clammy.

'I've sad news.' Her voice is uneven. 'The home-help phoned. Your mother died in her sleep an hour ago...' She leans towards me and extends her hand. 'I can't tell you how sorry I am. I knew her a long time ago.'

The blood is leaving my head so I put it between my knees. The swirling green and black of the floor tile reminds me of this morning when I vomited on the car park tarmac. It seems so long ago now.

'You poor dear. Mary will get you a nice cup of tea.' She squeezes my shoulder. 'You take all the time you want. I'll fill out your prescription and order a taxi.' Her eyes glisten as she walks towards the door. 'You're not in a fit state to drive.'

Having forced down the hot sweet liquid, I sit and wait. I feel calm and floating, as if I'm no longer in my body. Mary's granny gives me my tablets. I leave them on the chair beside me. A taxi beeps. I stumble outside. On the path in front of the florist potted tulips are opening their leaves leaking colour; they are red, darker towards the stem. I can see every bright vein in their leaves.

My thoughts force me to a place at the edge of memory where I have always avoided going, where I am small, lonely and tired.

It's the middle of the night. Noel is bawling. I'm leaning over his cot pressing on his back and pushing his head into the mattress. His little legs kick convulsively but there's no sound...

As I sit into the taxi, I remember that I've left my medication, what Mother used to call 'Joan's calming pills', behind me on a chair.

'Where to loveen?' the driver puts his hand on the gear handle and studies me in his rear view mirror.

Shoulders hunched, I clench and unclench my fists.

From Crannóg 31

Sixth Class

Gary King

With your permanent smirk
you stood at the blackboard
weighing up the hilarity of life.

Were you a fun guy?
No! you were just brilliant!
A mastermind – I would say.

Ruler of the tuck shop,
MC of the school concerts, football coach, keyboard player
'Mr. All Rounder' – those parents eat out of your hand.

Then the boy with the butter stains in his copy
you got him, then exposed him
to give the savage little arena another freak

Like a clever prosecutor
you held up the evidence
and reduced the testimony of the guilty – to babble.

Unlike my fourth class Himmler, you had no desire for black
sellotaped canes.
Verbal methods were more complete, in this, the Sardonic
Principality
of comic books, occasional homework and orange *Yamaha*
amplifiers.

Could I ever forget those ABBA afternoons?
Your favourite group, the words typed for all the class to sing
On a joyous Tuesday in the lent of 1976.

Oh, can't you hear me darling, can't you hear me SOS
would travel out into the corridors, the cloakroom, the grubby staffroom,
over to the freezing toilets with twenty numbered cubicles,
where 12 went straight to 14 as number 13 was not permitted to go on a door.
You'd probably now say *never mind that vocation bullshit*.
At that age I never heard of 'Cynicism'.
But I thank you for teaching me about the 'hilarity of life'.

From Crannóg 5

The Castle
Eileen Ní Shuilleabháin

(On visiting Clare Island, summer 2015)

Night straddles hemispheres
hinged between sleep and dawn.
Grey castle rain stained
rises like a requiem.
This was your house.
Settled in this silent land
Clew Bay misted and tangled in your fists.
I rest against your walls,
winds caw like a crow
Iron centuries leaning against my darkening bones.

I know this dream
fluid where I lose my voice
like a child.
Stammering ahead
slow and luscious.
I play among your ruins
stony peaks scaffold
the scuffed hillside.
Blue foxes gnaw at the roots of things.

I hear your ancient heart beat
caught in a snare.
The moon
remembering your pagan heart
the stars
their delinquent daughter.

From Crannóg 42

The Speed Of Sound
Ciarán Parkes

Slower than the speed of light, much slower than
a speeding bullet, its effect is seen
when a child falls and there's a gap between
his falling and his cry as if the world
had been paused then started up again.
Sometimes slower still, the cry creeps on
silently, to catch him years from then.

From Crannóg 31

The Irish Summer, 2018
Ruth Quinlan

There was an unexpected scarcity,
an absence of water in this country.
We, the waterlogged folk, a people
of knitted jumpers pearled with drizzle,
muck-spattered wellies in sucking fields,
cloud-banked skies and bursting heavens,
a thousand fond expressions for rain,
fumbled with the language of drought.

The reservoirs were drained out, empty,
silverfish scuttling in shadows
chasing tastes of tidemarks.
The umbilical cord to liquid severed,
we lived like lesser gods, suppressing
yearnings to lick the walls of caves
for a tongue-slick of moisture,
to retreat from the glare and hide
like troglodytes, do anything
to stop the frying
like over-stuffed sausages,
greased and salted with our own sweat.

From Crannóg 49

The People Who Named The Places
Tony O'Dwyer

The names of the land show the heart of the race;
They move on the tongue like the lilt of a song.
                    John Hewitt, *Ulster Names*

I see them point with declamatory sticks,
Scribbling in the air the land's chirography,
The names falling like seed to the clean ground.

First they named the mountains:
Sliabh an Óir, Sliabh Bán ... Then they climbed.

From there they issued these decrees:
That would be *The Isle of Heather*, here
The Wooded Hillside, this *The Hazel Glen*.

But they used the older tongue – more suited
To describe than merely nominate the land's heart –
Inis Fraoch, Leitir Coille, Gleann na Sceach.

Earlier they had decided that to name the land
Would make it easier for all to navigate,
And on return to tell where they had been.

Deep within, too, a vague dream
That the words might find their way
To some future map, carried by the gods of place.

But now the land's topography is hidden
Where the dust of history lies heaviest.

We've drawn on it with meagre sticks
A meaningless cartography:
Inishfree, Letterkelly, Glenaskeagh.

From Crannóg 31

Transients
Geraldine Mills

i.m Eva Saulitis

The woman moves away from where
she was made, to Prince William Sound.
Something about it smells of home. She stays.

Each spring she watches the bay for the orcas,
named after the mountain that welcomes them,
sees them along the shoreline, seal-hunting.

She gets to know them,
voice by voice, tail by tail.
She is in her element, theirs.

Soon she learns that in this place
of islets and exposed rock,
of dripping forests, cloud-layers

that there are more ways to wipe out
a species than to harpoon them:
Let the tanker sidle in,

let it bleed the blood of fossils
into the Sound and see,
how in twenty years, not one orca pup born.

From Crannóg 50

Tulca
Aideen Henry

Irish for wave, gust, gush, outpouring, flood, deluge.

Sacrum and sternum in gold,
both keystones, crowns of arches,
reciprocal.

They embrace pressure from each side,
disseminate impetus, uncoil movement,
crossways

up through the body from the kicking foot
or down from the throwing arm
symmetrically

through the body when the butterfly kick
pitches head and winged arms
up out of water like a rising angel.

From Crannóg 35

Stealing Boyfriends

Aoibheann McCann

I settled into the beige armchair and took out the NOW magazine. Katie Price's new husband had been caught cheating again. The door opened on the hour and a middle-aged woman, sniffling into a tissue, slumped past me and went down the stairs.

Susan, the counsellor, was wearing a ridiculous asymmetrical cardigan with matching beads and a flowing skirt that clashed with her toddler-style shoes. She still didn't seem to know that Lady Diana had died and taken that hairstyle to the grave. I went in and sat down. The huddle of woollen-haired dolls on the windowsill hadn't been moved since the week before.

'Stephanie, how have you been?'

'Good, thanks Susan.' I nodded compliantly and tried to look sad.

'We did some powerful work in the last session.'

'Yes, I have been thinking about my father a lot in the week,' I sighed, shaking my head.

'Well that's understandable. I'd like us to do an exercise today, if that's OK with you.'

'Whatever you think, Susan, you're the expert.'

She smiled, got up from her chair, walked to the corner of the room, lifted a wooden stool and placed it between us to make a triangle. Sitting back down, she held her hand out towards the stool like a lacklustre magician's assistant. 'I want you to imagine that your father is sitting on this stool, Stephanie. I want you to talk to him, to tell him what's happened and why you're here.'

I took a deep breath. 'Well Daddy, you're not looking so great,' I said.

Susan didn't bat an eye when I looked over at her, just nodded me back in the direction of the empty stool.

'Well Daddy, I suppose you've been watching me since you died? That'd be typical you. But you can hardly judge, can you? Yep, affair with my boss. I'm just like you, am I not Daddy?' I was really getting into it at that stage. 'I started out stealing Twixes and now I've graduated to men. But now work have sent me here, Daddy. Everyone hates me in the office, they're glaring at me, Daddy, they've hidden my favourite cup...' Then I started screeching and put my head between my hands. I sobbed for as long as I could get away with. I had discovered this was the best way to while away these mandated sessions. Eventually, as she always did, Susan leaned across with a tissue.

'Well done, Stephanie,' she whispered, 'now with your permission I'd like to examine what you said to your father.'

'OK,' I sniffed.

'You mentioned stealing, Stephanie, can you tell me a bit more about that?'

'Oh, I used to steal things when I was a kid, buttons from school, money from my mother's purse, those sorts of things, the usual kid stuff.'

'And why did you stop? Did your father catch you?'

'He hit me with his belt but that didn't stop me. I got caught by the security guard in Boots.'

'And were you prosecuted?'

'No, they let me off with it because of my father's death. I was very lucky.'

'OK. So I'd like to bring you back to the act of stealing. So you simply stopped after getting caught?'

'Just couldn't do it after that, to be honest. I lost the nerve, and my mother was so upset.'

'Your mother, yes, we'll come back to her, but you said you feel you stole this man, Jeff, your current boss?'

'I suppose I was always attracted to attached men.'

'And are there any attached men in your life at the moment?'

I thought of Jonesy. 'No,' I said, 'I think I've learned my lesson, getting caught in the office and all that.'

'Well, that's positive I suppose. Now we are drawing close to the end of our session, so I'd like you to think about your addiction to drama more in the coming week so we can return to it next time.'

'Addiction to drama?'

She tilted her head. 'I suggest that the affair was a substitute for your inability to face up to the circumstances of your father's death; a compulsion to repeat the drama so you could control it, as such. Your father being found dead in bed with your teacher, that was a very traumatic experience for a young woman just reaching puberty.'

'Oh,' I said, 'I see what you mean,' I was nodding vigourously as if this was all so insightful and I had never read a fucking pop psychology book or a Marie Claire article in my life.

'So, how will you mind yourself this week, Stephanie?'

'Mind myself?'

'Well, we discussed ways of relaxing, have you tried any of my suggestions?'

'Well, no. I thought about what you said but I'm more of a magazine person than a hot bath person.'

'Oh yes, I saw you reading a gossip magazine in the waiting room. That's an unusual choice for a woman like you.'

'A woman like me?'

'Well, from what you've told me in the last three sessions, you are a very intelligent woman Stephanie, you did very well at college, you walked straight into a job after your A-Levels, you were headhunted for the position you are in now.'

'I just like to switch off.'

'Well, I wouldn't exactly call these gossip magazines switching off, Stephanie. Given your life history, it's more like switching on.'

'Oh. I see what you mean.'

'Perhaps a *Psychologies* magazine or an *Oprah* would be more conducive to relaxing. And you could even try to read one in a hot bath.'

'Oh,' I said, 'well thank you Susan, I will think about it in the week.'

I walked out smiling, straight past the next client who was engrossed in her phone. Outside, I dumped the magazine in the nearest bin and opened a few buttons on my blouse.

Jonesy was there waiting, two empty coffees on the table beside him. He jumped up to kiss me on the cheek. His eyebrows were bushier than I remembered but I still lingered just that little bit longer than was business-like. His eyes wandered down to my cleavage and back, as if they had a life of their own.

'Sorry I'm late,' I said, 'how's Alexandria, was she asking for me?

He looked at me blankly.

'Alexandra, the receptionist. You know she said I stole her boyfriend? That's why I left to be honest, couldn't be bothered with her bullshit.'

'Typical,' he said, rolling his eyes, 'as if we can just be stolen, what is this supposed to be, the reverse of the middle ages where bands of marauding women steal men for themselves and haul them back to their lairs?'

'I could steal you if I wanted to.'

He laughed.

'Challenge accepted, prepare to be stolen.'

'Well, Jill might object but go ahead and try,' he said.

'Anyway. How's things at Legal and Pacific?'

'Same old, same old. How long is it since you left?'

'Three months.'

'Mad. So how's the new job?'

'Oh you know, more money, more perks.'

'So what brings you back out here, you're not trying to poach our clients are you?'

I laughed, 'Can't say, haven't finished negotiations, top secret I'm afraid.' I looked at my phone. 'Sorry J, I have to run for my train.'

'So soon? But I thought you were going to stick me in your bag or something?'

'It will happen when you least expect it! Great seeing you though, if you are you ever up in the actual city give me a shout.'

'If they let me though the barricades I'll let you know,' he said, getting up to hug me goodbye.

I stepped in closer, lingering on the smell of his neck, breathing him in, he smelled of shaving cream and just a trace of sweat. I ran my index finger slowly across his neck and left.

From: "AlexJones" <jones.alex@legalandpacific.com >
Date: February 5, 2015 at 14:22:41 GMT
To: "Stephanie Marks" <cindybeale2@gmail.com>
Subject: Hi from Croydon

Great to see you again Steph,
You still living in Dulwich? I will actually be in the Peckham office at a meeting on Wednesday, why don't we meet up after (if I get out of Peckham alive …)? Where's good?
Jonesy

From: "StephanieMarks" <cindybeale2@gmail.com>
Date: February 5, 2015 at 15:25:35 GMT
To: "Alex Jones" <jones.alex@legalandpacific.com >
Subject: Hi from Croydon

Great to see you too,
Oh brilliant I am just a walk from there. Why don't you call in after and we'll go on to my local? What time do you think you'll be finished?
Look forward to it! (Directions below!)
Steph
https://www.google.ie/maps/place/Dulwich,+22b. Green.+Road/@53.2918,-9.0901687,17z/data=!3m1!4b1!4m5!3m4!1s0x485b9 6655d58c08b:0x61ef3811d1626ed9!8m2!3d53.29179 69!4d-9.0880108

I smiled and allowed the thrill to start moving up my thighs as the train pulled into London Bridge Station. I rang my beautician for an appointment.

The red bumps from the Hollywood wax had disappeared nicely by Wednesday morning. I went to work until lunchtime, then feigned a headache and went home to prepare. I had another shower, left my hair damp but redid my Rock Star Red lipstick. I slid on the red kimono

Jeff had bought me, fresh from its expensive navy box embossed with silver Japanese writing: maybe the kimono had been his final undoing, maybe the very expensive receipt had led his wife to us in the office that night. Led her to the sight of the back of his head between my legs. I had stared at her triumphantly, the sight of her horrified face making me moan louder, clench my thighs tighter around his ears. I had waited until he finished. When he rose up and tried to kiss me on the mouth, I told him. He had lurched after her, grey-faced, fumbling at his belt.

When the doorbell rang, I turned to muss my hair in the mirror, and widened my eyes for my surprise-face, you've-caught-me-unawares face, I'd-forgotten-you-were-calling face. But it wasn't Jonesy. It was a tall black-haired woman with a beige mac on. She'd been crying. She stepped onto the threshold, hissing at me, and there was nothing pretend about my surprise.

I tried to close the door in her face but she grabbed me by the hair and pulled me forwards. I reached up for her wrist, but her fury pushed me to the pavement; she ripped at my kimono with her other hand and my left breast fell out of the flimsy bra underneath. Her foot came down towards my stomach, but I grabbed her ankle and she toppled down beside me. I was aware that people had started gathering; there were flashes as we fought. Camera phones came closer but no one tried to stop her. Then someone grabbed her arms and pulled her up roughly,

'Steph? What the fuck's going on?'

It was Jonesy. He had his arms wrapped around the black-haired woman, she was shouldering him and screaming in a bid to get back at me. The camera phones turned back to me as I struggled to cover myself with the kimono and sit up at the same time.

Then I heard the sirens.

'Psycho bitch!' I shouted as they pushed her head down into the back of the police car. I read the policeman's card and thought about what I'd wear to visit the police station.

Jonesy guided me into the house and shut the door against the crowd. He went to the bathroom and brought back some wet tissue and indicated where I should wipe my mouth. There was blood.

'What the fuck is going on Steph?'

'One of those marauding women you were talking about Jonesy,' I said, 'though you got it slightly wrong, they come for the women who take their men, that's when they use full force.'

'So you stole her boyfriend or something?'

'Probably,' I said, 'there's been so many. Who knows? But that's why you were here, right, to be stolen?'

He looked at me blankly. 'Look Stephanie if you're sure you're OK, I have to go.'

'I know you felt the sparks between us but it's fine,' I said, 'I've got to get ready anyway.'

'Ready for what?'

'The journalists, I'm sure they'll turn up when the video goes viral.'

When he was gone, I gulped down a glass of wine, then returned to the bathroom to fix my make-up. I pulled at the small tear in the kimono, ripped it down a little further. Then I returned to the living room to wait. Walking towards the black TV screen, I caught my reflection. I blew myself a kiss.

From Crannóg 50

The Day of Ashes
Rita O'Donoghue

Always a double-edged sword, the Lenten promise
hung over you, cajoled you into strict sobriety.
Forty days of abstinence, dying for a drink,
Each bead of sweat a station in your cross
taking it hard to be so full of weakness.
Not for you the chest-beating path to righteousness
sackcloth of public purification and penance
that Wednesday morning saw you prepare:
clean out the ashes, light the fire, make the porridge,
wait for the news, then slip back to bed
a marked man in a sleepened state,
you quietly found your way back to grace.

From Crannóg 18

Under the Arch

Esther Murbach

Under the ancient Arch
a pale face hangs in the dark
like a pinched moon
on a distorted sky

This must be the guy
who walks a miniature dog
each day
along the shore
from Claddagh and back
if weather permits

Today it didn't
he went out anyway

In a bulge of his wet coat
on his chest
nestles the tiny creature
which nearly got blown away
spinning on a long leash
like a misshapen kite on a string
toppling over instead of flying
in an angry squall

He's ever so sorry
to have put doggie through this
used him as an excuse
to get a breath of fresh air
too fresh as it turned out
even for himself

The wife had stayed home
she always stayed home
having things to look after
seven four-legged dwarfs
to be exact

But she wasn't Snow White
destiny had denied her a prince
the poison of some malevolent apple
got stuck in her throat for good
making her barren

Instead of sons and daughters
she raises Chihuahuas

When the rain subsides
the husband reluctantly
leaves the shelter of the Arch
ambling back home
to hot soup and dog food

From Crannóg 36

Scúba Thumadóireacht i gConamara

Pat Folan

Culaith uiscedhíonach rubair fite fuaite fúm,
An fharraige fuar fhliuch ag fanacht liom,
Titim siar amach as mo bháidín,
Feicim spéir, ansin an tsáile ghlas.
Bolgán bheaga ag éalú suas,
Mise ag dul go tóin poill,
Síos go grinneall,
Is ann atá mé ar mo shámh.
Le buidéal aer ar mo dhroim,
Agus gliondar i mo gcroí,
Mé ag féachaint ar an dúlra báite,
Le lampa láidir solais chun go bhfeicfidh me an tslí.
Is iomaí uair a chuimhnigh mé,
Ar an dream a tháinig romhainn,
Ní fhaca siadsan an áilleacht seo,
Mura rabhadar i gcontúirt bá.
Is beag taitneamh a bhain siad as,
Bhí rudaí eile dá gcrá,
Is mór an peaca nach raibh scúba ceaptha fós,
Nach acu a bheadh an lá.

From Crannóg 13

Drunk– I Bunk With Malice ...

John Martin

Drunk – I bunk with malice.
Pissed – I ping pong dolly
mixed surprise in eyes that
hold no longer useful love –
nor its magnifying glaze.

Later – I hear the tempered
season calling *"sting"* – bring
this bastard to his knees.
The vast expanse of holy
Heaven orders more to drink!!!

From Crannóg 6

44

Vilenica Cave: Closing Ceremony, Vilenica Festival; Slovenia

Miceál Kearney

We gather – like the leaves will soon –
schizophrenics from all over the world.
Clouds crack'd: a shimmering spectacle.
Day and Night chase each other about.
Captivating in leaps and bounds, we interpret
and rotate. Celestial bodies, casting shadows
on individual leaves of surrounding saplings.

The dancers disappear.
A hand reappears, beckons
us down
            to
                  the
                        depths,
                  we
            descend
      the
steps.

Where we find the 2 lovers dancing,
this time, with the Sun and the Moon
and music soliloquys around them.
Fixated as the stalactites I stop.

This is where they used to come to read,
when verbs were illegal and metaphors
a death sentence. The cold would mute
to the communists' ear. I am uncomfortable,
the wren.

From Crannóg 36

Wallace Hartley's Last Moments Aboard The Titanic

Susan Millar Dumars

for Michael Diskin

And what has made your life
worth living?
As the deck pitches
and water reaches
past your knees
and the sky is sharp
with stars, but not one
that can lead you home.
What has made this life
yours?

Don't look for God, but
yourself;
if He is anywhere,
He's in your answer.
The tune you play
as the ship goes down.

Longer than the screams, the prayers,
the crack and gush and groan,
longer than the pop of signal flares,

we will hear your song.

From Crannóg 30

Welcome

Fred Johnston

i.m. Judee Sill

Now is the toll-booth
with its basket for spare change
yellow barrier like a border crossing
and beyond, the last run home

Now the foot pressing out
a glad acceleration
eyed by neon watchtowers –
the night territories avoided, passed
far small lights over black fields
mark where jaded others undress
TVs turn themselves off
'phones perish unanswered

Now too the tunnel
entered like a rape –
under the river's skirts
a fingering of headlights, groan of gears
After this, the crass familiarity
of sniffling rubber on a bed of gravel:
all day we've waited for this

Now the house so predictably dead,
rain prostitutes itself
in the drains, the smell of sex
rising out of the wet gardens
the engine cooling, calming
out of breath. I'm home. Welcome me.

From Crannóg 46

On Being Arrested with Other Greenham Women for Entering a Restricted Military Zone

Margaretta Darcy

A diluted landscape made into mud tracks by the
military.
Such beauty such green spaces
hemmed in by byelaws.
Our eyes are put into boxes:
nowhere to look
except into the eyes of
law & order officers.

From Crannóg 5

You Shouldn't Have To Kill Your Mother
Maureen Gallagher

Once this dog in our neighbourhood began to behave very strangely, for some unknown reason. You'd see it on the green chasing its tail for hours and hours. All us kids would stand and gawk at it going around and around. Round and round. Day after day, all day long. Nothing we did would distract it. Eventually I suppose it had to have exhausted itself and lain down to sleep. But we never saw it. All we ever saw was the poor mutt chasing its tail.

Mama was a bit like that dog that day coming up to Christmas. Like a whirlwind, flying around and around. One minute on the mobile, the next writing notes, the next bunging things into a plastic shopping bag. Then back on the mobile. We just watched, Ellie and me. Well, Ellie was only three at the time; she began to whimper for food. What else!

Porridge, she demanded.

Mama throwing stuff onto the table: slices of pan loaf, half a banana, a dirty carrot, milk, beans left over from yesterday's dinner. A bowl of jelly. You wouldn't know if this was supposed to be breakfast or dinner.

Next thing we knew we were in the Fiesta, on our way.

'Where we going, Mama,' Ellie wanted to know. Mama said nothing. We were on a journey but where? It was Tuesday and I was supposed to be at school. Today I wanted to be at school. It was the last day before the holidays and there could be a party.

But Mama wasn't driving anywhere near school. We passed the shopping centre all done up for Christmas, past the big tree at Wood Quay, sparkly with white lights going on and off. Past the town hall where our school had put on Toad of Toad Hall for the Christmas play. Me as Toad. Up to the traffic lights. Then the hospital. Were we sick?

Mama parked and all of us running at full speed up to the front entrance. Ellie complaining that her feet were sore. In our rush out the door no one had thought of putting shoes on the child. Plus she was still in her jumpsuit and I could see a big snot running down her nose. I gave it a swipe with my sleeve and picked her up. Once inside Ellie struggled free and made a dash over to – wouldn't you know! – the fairy lights. Mama yanked her back. Over with the lot of us to the desk. Ellie started to cry at the top of her voice.

'Is this the unit?' Mama asked.

'Who are you looking for?'

'A social worker.'

'Do you have an appointment?'

'I need to see a social worker.'

'Have you been referred?'

Ellie was screeching now, pulling at a forty-five degree angle away from Mama. Like she was on a mission to get away.

'Please, I need...'

'I'm sorry, you can't just...'

Mama wheeling us back out at high speed, Ellie protesting at full volume. On another journey, this time out the coast road. Mama driving like mad. Driving. Driving. It looked like we were heading out to Silver Strand like we used to do in summer holidays. Before Dada left.

I missed Dada. We didn't see him much now. He'd been great with helping me when my racer bike got a flat tyre. Which was all the time. Or if the dynamo needed fixing. Mama was useless at all that. Plus she was crying all the time so she hardly ever heard me. When I asked her why Dada left home, all she said was she told him to take himself off with his floozie and good riddance. "What's a floozie?" I said.

It started to rain, big fat drops blotting the windscreen.

We didn't take the left turn off to Silver Strand. On we went. Further on. Past Barna and the Twelve Pins. The Twelve Pins was where we'd gone two years before on the day of my First Holy Communion. For a big slap up. Gran and Uncle Jim with us too. Uncle Jim was really my Granda but he liked us kids to call him Uncle Jim. It was a mighty feed, I remembered that. Out past Spiddal. I could see a sign for *An Gaeltacht*. I'd been to the Gaeltacht once on a school trip. We bought these big sweet rocks in a shop called Padraigín's, that lasted for days.

On and on and on. Not many houses now. Just stones and walls.

In the end we took a left where I could see a sign for an airport. Were we taking a plane somewhere? But we had no cases with us and Ellie was still in her peejay's. We went flying down this side road and pulled to a stop at the end of a pier. Ellie still whingeing. A fisherman was pulling a rope out of the water. He gave us the once over. Then back to his tugging, coiling the rope as it came up. When he came to the last part he fastened it around an iron hook that was buried in concrete. One last look over his shoulder and off up to the road. We all watched him turn the corner and he was gone.

'Mama, I want to go home,' I said.

The sky was winter dark now and giant waves were smashing up against the pier, sending huge jets of spray all over the car.

'Mama ...'

But Mama was just sitting there. Staring out at the cold sea. She didn't seem to hear me. Ellie's crying had risen a few notches and she was bawling her head off now. To distract her, I turned around and started to talk about Santa and all the things he would bring her on Christmas Eve.

'Ellie, Santa is on his sleigh right now on his way with tons of presents for you and me.'

Ellie looked at me, pink-eyed.

'He has a baby doll for you, and let's see, what's this else?'

'A pram,' piped up Ellie, tears forgotten.

'That's right ... and I'm getting a Nintendo and ...'

The scream took us by complete surprise, made us both jump. An out-of-this-world scream that drowned out even the sound of the sea. We sat there stunned. A long time. Us just sitting. And Mama screaming. Then the sobbing. Sobbing. Sobbing. I put my arm around her shoulders. I was big for my age; I was able to reach up.

'Mama...' I said. Her thin body was shuddering like a washing machine.

'Sorry, son,' she said in between sobs.

Another wave crashed over us.

'I'm supposed to be at school, Mama.' But she just kept on crying. 'Mama, are you supposed to be at work?'

After a long while she said, 'Twenty of us were let go yesterday, son.'

Mama worked in Roche's furniture store. She said the boss came in at five o clock and closed it down. Just like that. Told them all to get their things and be out of the place in twenty minutes.

'It's the downturn,' he said.

It was on TV all the time. About how everything was in a bad way, in recession and all that. I didn't pay too much heed. It was hard to understand anyway.

I don't exactly know how long we stayed there right up at the end of the pier, looking out at the ugly sea, waves whooshing up all around us. When I finally persuaded Mama to reverse up to the road, I remember feeling really afraid she wouldn't steer us back up the pier properly – her driving wasn't hectic – and that we'd slip off the side and end up in the water, the three of us done for.

She inched back. I kept looking out the side window. Just in case. Once we got very close to the edge. Another time the car jerked to a stop. Mama started up again. Then we were on the road, on our way home.

Back at the flat and Ellie crying again, a monotonous gripe. The place was a kip. The fireplace full of burnt-out papers. Ellie's toys all over the place. A broken brush, Mama had tried to fix, still in the middle of the floor. Mama started to scream like before. She collapsed onto her knees beside where Ellie was sitting near the kitchen door. Began to punch the sofa. She kept on punching as if she was trying to get all the dust out. Her screams tailed off into a kind of animal moan. A wounded animal like you'd see on the Discovery channel. I took hold of Ellie's hand and tried to drag her away but she wouldn't budge, pulled her hand back stubbornly. Continued on with her whining like an old crock of an engine revving over.

I crept upstairs to my room and closed the door quietly. Very quietly. Crept into bed. I tried to block out the howls from below. After a while, how long? the crying stopped. Suddenly. No sound at all now. Alert as a warrior from my *Sabre-Tooth Killer* comic, I listened as hard as I could. The silence was even worse than the cries.

Footsteps on the landing. I kept my eyes fixed on the door. Waiting for the knob to turn.

It turned.

Afterwards, the house full of people.

'A double tragedy,' someone said. But I couldn't take it in. *A double tragedy.*

And the Gardai. With their questions. Questions. Words. I was sinking under an avalanche of words, I was sinking and the only thing I could clearly make out was someone – was it me? – saying, 'You shouldn't have to kill your mother.' A case of self-defence, they said, the woman was clearly out of her mind.

She gave you life, you owe it to her to survive. Of course, you're not working it out clearly like that when there's a pillow over your face. You just fight back. Resist. It's hard to resist a grown woman when you're only nine but luckily I was big for my age. Strong.

From Crannóg 37

Ursula

Michelle Coyne

The cat is on to me. She's watching me balefully through the patio doors, and I'm watching her right back. I bring the joint to my lips and suck sharply in. I imagine the sweet tendrils invading every space, each alveolar pocket, inside my chest, licking up against capillary walls and entering my bloodstream. After a pause, I part my lips and let the smoke make its lazy escape. The cat drops her head before slinking down from the back step. I watch her tail flick out of view and am reminded of Ursula.

The wicker chair creaks in protest as I curl my feet under me. 'Ursula,' I say to nobody. Her name feels alien on my tongue, the very same tongue that used to trace constellations between the freckles on her stomach. Time has been careless with my love.

I try to imagine her walking into the room and sitting next to me, but it's pointless. All that's left of her in my head is a scatter of useless fragments. Hundreds of them. But still not enough to resurrect the memory of an actual real human being. Not even one who called me her girlfriend for four years.

It's funny though, the pieces that are still with me. I can't find any pattern as to why these are the things I committed to indelible memory. I can see her tomcat crawl across the sheets, for instance, and her soft-lidded mascara smudged stare from between my thighs. I can hear the gentle nasal huffs she made whilst reading, with a different tone for each thought, or emotion, or christ-knows-what. I can't remember her scent, or our combined scent, but I'm certain I'd recognise it in an instant if I ever happened upon it again. It's bolted up tight somewhere, kept safe for an occasion that's never going to arrive.

I can picture the back of her head in brutal detail, though. That familiar dark rooted blonde, stuck askew from yet another night lying awake across the bed from me. And those mirrored half moons of freckles on her beaten down shoulders. She left without a word; there was nothing left to say, but there was still the half-life fade of her footsteps on the long gravel path before I closed the door. It was always going to end that way, with me as the victor, and her as the defeated, right from the very beginning. We both knew it, and we both still chose it. Fucked up, really.

The hurt faded quickly at the time, but I'm sore now thinking about her. I mean, I burned for Ursula, and now I can't even make her solid in my memories. She's just a faceless cloud of features whose loss I'll never be done mourning. Same as anyone, I suppose, but you'd think I might have learned my lesson. Another toke, and I let it scorch my useless tongue and worthless lips, allow it to pollute and poison me for a moment before I let it all go again.

His key-fumble in the lock startles me from my reflecting. I really should dump the last puff out the window, but I'm so tired of lying. When he comes in he says nothing, but his head quirks to one side to indicate his disappointment in me. I try to care, I really do, but I have enough disappointment in myself to deal with, without taking his on too. And the cat can go fuck herself.

Around the corner and out of sight his keys collide with the countertop. 'Did you manage to get the avocados? ' His voice is trained into softness.

'Yeah. They're in the bowl.' I pinch the butt of the joint and open the patio door to go outside and gulp some fresh air while he pummels the avocados into guacamole. I lean against the damp block wall and let its cold invade my skin through the thin fabric of my t-shirt. A thought occurs to me, and I can't stub it out, because that's the way it goes with the truth. Someday I'll be his Ursula.

From Crannóg 36

Waving Goodbye to Leonard Cohen

Patricia McAdoo

The clock on the dash reads 4.30 am and I believe it. It's Mick's Beetle. Everything works as it should. We are driving towards the airport. A frill of daffodils lines the central reservation, a rare show of welcome to the tourists. I haven't brushed my furry teeth. I haven't shaved. This is not the way I planned to say goodbye to Leonard Cohen.

Mick, on the other hand, is humming. It is 1983 but already Mick is a man not of his generation. He drinks water between drinks. Mick looks after himself. What's more the bastard's face is as smooth as a baby's arse and there is a faint smell of woody after-shave.

He has set this whole thing up. With Leonard. Or his agent. I lean my head against the window and breathe cool air from the ventilator. The hangover starts to come to life, kicking in with gusto. I moan very softly.

Mick parks in the short term car park and I totter after him through the swishing doors. The place is empty except for a lone cleaning lady.

'Joe said to go on up so that's what we'll do, yeah?' Mick says.

I nod and slouch along the shiny corridor after Mick, my hands gripping the pockets of my denim jacket. I wish I'd worn my jumper but the smell of smoke on it turned my stomach. Mick takes the stairs two at a time. Two men in black suits stand near the top talking. They both have walkie-talkies to their ears. The taller one raises his hand as Mick grins and says: 'Joe, my man.'

Joe does not smile. 'We have a problem.'

Mick goes into a huddle in a corner with Joe, which strikes me as unnecessary since there's no one else there. Mick nods as if he knows all about what's happening which he doesn't. This is a very big deal for Mick. This is a very big deal for me too. I slump into a row of chairs, cool my throbbing head against the metal frame and close my eyes.

A man in a crisp cream linen suit sits down opposite me and I wonder why. The whole of the departure lounge is empty. I lean forward. It is Leonard Cohen.

'Leonard. Mr. Cohen.' I hear my voice crack into a nervous whisper.

'Mick.'

'No. I'm Kev.' I say. 'Mick's over there.'

'Ah. A slight misunderstanding.'

'How are you?'

'I'm good, Kev. How are you?'

'Ok. A bit of a head. The gig was fantastic. Amazing.'

'Thank you, Kev. I really appreciate that.'

Leonard Cohen has a lovely cashmere jumper draped across the shoulders of his cream linen suit. It is soft and I rest my very sore eyes on its soothing blueness. A cold wind seems to blow through the departure lounge. Air conditioning. It feels like the Gulag Archipelago.

'You want my sweater, Kevin?'

I pull my denim jacket tight and close some buttons. 'I'm fine.'

'Are you in the industry?'

'No.'

'You're not? But I thought...'

'I'm here with Mick.'

'I see. And you're not with AMI?'

'No. I'm a teacher.'

'Mhhm.'

'Yes.'

'What?'

'Huh?'

'I'm sorry. What is it that you teach?'

'Everything. I teach first class. Boys.'

'Like grade school?'

'Yeah.' I shrug. 'It's just a job.' I say. This is the line I often use when I talk to girls I don't know for the first time and then I do the shrug.

'That doesn't sound good... "a job".' Leonard draws imaginary italics. His nails are polished.

'Not too many of them around at the moment.' My face is set in what I hope is a serious, considered look. 'Gotta make a living.' I want Leonard to feel my pain...draw back the bandages from my misspent life and lay them bare on the smooth glass topped table.

'I see.' Leonard looks pensive, his lean tanned face in quiet repose.

'The whole country's goin' down the tubes. Slap bang in the middle of a recession.'

Leonard frowns slightly. 'That's too bad.'

I think he is beginning to get it. 'Oh, it's ok. It's just a recession.'

'No jobs?'

'Nope. You kinda get used to it. Half the country's on the dole.'

'But you teach.'

'Yeah. It's either that or take the next plane out.' I look down at the table, conscious of Leonard's eyes. I am keenly aware of his interest in the conversation. I just wish I was firing on all four cylinders.

'Ever thought about doing that?'

'Yeah. Everyone thinks about it. There's a joke doing the rounds: will the last person leaving the country please turn off the lights?' I grin.

Leonard frowns. 'That bad?'

'Yeah.' I resume my intense serious look. I stare hard at Leonard in what I hope is an earnest intelligent way; try to set my jaw to be open, honest. 'It about sums it up all right.'

'But you stay?'

'Well...yeah...I have something.'

'Something you want?'

'I dunno.'

'How long you been teaching?'

'Five years.'

'Really? And you can't tell yet?'

'It has its moments. There's a lot of time when it's boring.'

Somewhere on the landing the vacuum cleaner circles.

'What age are you, Kev? If its not too impertinent to ask.'

'Twenty-seven. But really I could be any age. Having a pension is everything —you can feel sixty even if you're really young.' I wonder whether I know any more facts if we go further down the economy road. 'It's daft but like that's just the way it is ...' I lean back, pleased with how clearly I have managed to describe the heartbreak of a whole generation.

Leonard looks out the window but all that's there is an empty car park. 'Anyway, right now you're taking a holiday some place?'

'God, no!'

'Oh. So ... what are you doing here?'

'Mick brought me ... we were at the gig ... and he promised to bring me out so we could say goodbye.'

Leonard's eyes sag a little. He takes a packet of Marlboro from his inside pocket and offers me one. He produces a gold lighter. We lean back and smoke in silence. Me and Leonard Cohen, just shooting the breeze.

'So it's Mick that's leaving then?'

'What? Oh no. Mick is staying put. We're heading down to Lisdoon after this. Lisdoonvarna. Folk festival. Me and Mick do all the gigs around the country during the summertime.'

A faint sigh escapes from Leonard. 'I thought you said you were saying goodbye.'

'Yeah. To you.'

Leonard's eyes watch me through the smoky haze. 'It's five am? Right?'

'Yes. About five.'

'And you drove out here with Mick so you could say goodbye to me?'

'Yeah.'

'Why?'

'Because...it's important.'

'That's very cool.'

'We're ... I've got every record.'

'Well and so... here we are.' A small yawn escapes from Leonard. He gets up slowly. 'Kevin, the plane is ready to taxi.' He throws his cigarette in the ashtray. 'It's been a real pleasure, I must say, to connect with you like this. It's what I like about Dublin...people extend themselves on just a whim ... it's very good.'

'No bother.'

'It's been a real pleasure.'

'Goodbye, Kevin.'

'Goodbye, Mr ... Leonard.'

He begins to stroll away but he talks over his shoulder as he goes. 'You don't need to think about your pension, Kevin. You need to think about your life.'

He raises his right hand in a sort of casual 'so long' gesture, his soft sandals moving soundlessly across the great expanse of shiny floor. I watch until he is gone through a pair of glass doors.

Someone is tugging at my shoulder. 'Jesus, Kev. The state of you.'

I am smothered by the woodiness of Mick's aftershave.

'He's gone, Mick. He couldn't wait. I tried to get him over to have a word with you.'

'What are ya on about? What...are you stoned?'

'No.'

Mick has me by the shoulder. His narrowed eyes are jumping from side to side. 'You tripping?'

'No. I told ya.'

'Look, we might as well go. There's nothing happening here. Come all the way out for this crap ... Come on. Let's hit the road.'

'Ok.'

'So come on!' Mick is hopping from foot to foot. 'Let's get outa here. I'm freezing me balls off in this kip.'

I follow Mick out of the airport and into the morning sun. It feels so warm, cocooning us, carrying us along in its rays. The engine of the Beetle thunders into life and we head back down the road to town.

'He was really sound.'

'Who?'

'Leonard.'

Mick curses softly. 'Quit taking the piss. I'm not in the mood.'

'He was.'

'Jesus. What is with you? And what's with the smile? You look weird.'

'I can't help it. We talked about my situation. Like me being at a cross roads and everything.'

'You were asleep, ya dope.'

'He showed me, Mick. There's a way out of all this.'

'Jesus wept. This is all head stuff with you, Kevin. You gotta see a shrink soon.'

We drive in silence. The daffodils wave in the breeze. It is springtime. Everything is young and bursting with life. The springtime of my life.

'Mick, would you come to California with me?'

Mick slows the car and his voice slows too. He speaks each word clearly, the way I do with the little kids in first class, especially the thick ones.

'What hallucinogenic substance were you imbibing last night? You seemed fine on the way out.'

'Nothing. I took nothing. Would you?'

'For what?'

'Maybe go driving ... Route 66. Maybe play some music.'

'We're cat. We don't know the words of anything and you only know four chords.'

'We could improve.'

'This is all pipe dreams. Anyway I've got stuff going on here.'

'Maybe it's not. We've talked about it ... why don't we do it?'

'And live on what?'

'I'll cash in my pension.'

Mick looks across at me. 'You would? Just like that? Now I know you need a shrink.'

'I want to. I don't need a pension. I need a life.'

Mick gives me a sidelong look. 'Where d'ya get a line like that?'

'From Leon ... I'm gonna do it, Mick. With or without you.'

'I'm sorry I brought you out here.'

'Why?'

'Well, it's obvious, isn't it? We missed Cohen and the security guys were obnoxious and now ... I dunno ... you're acting like you've seen the Second Coming.' We drive on some more. 'Anyway,' Mick says, jerking his thumb to his side window, 'there's your last chance to say good-bye. That's him there.'

'Who?'

'His plane.'

'Stop.'

'What?'

'Stop the car.'

'Ah, jaysus.'

'Please.'

Mick screeches to a halt on the hard shoulder. I get out and zigzag through the honking commuters till I jump onto the central reservation. I look up. High above me a jumbo is streaking across the bay.

I raise my hand and wave, feeling a huge weight lift from me. Tooting car horns surround me. Someone rolls their window down and roars: 'Bye Byeeeeeee' and their laughter echoes after them.

But I am weightless. I am soaring free of Dublin. I can fly. So I wave on and on till all I can see is a thin bluish wisp, till my arm aches and my neck is sore from craning and my eyes have tears from squinting against the morning sun.

From Crannóg 25

What Somervell Saw
Sarah O'Toole

Everest - June 1924

And slowly they start to seem more far away
Two tiny specks above us climbing strong
We do not know what price we'll have to pay

Mallory decides this will be their day
They check their kit, take oxygen tanks along
And slowly they start to move farther away

It's more treacherous in the snow than on the clay
(A whole chunk of my oesophagus is gone)
We don't know yet what price they'll have to pay

Near the Second Step, a mist veils the display
Of their bravado, they'll be down before too long
But suddenly they start to seem so far away

The mountain's silence chokes us, hopes give way
Two days, we make a cross to tell what's wrong
And, oh, the awful price we've had to pay.

Did they reach the top? Well, who can say?
Poor Ruth, no husband, just a hero's song,
And they never let him die or climb away -
For Immortality - that's the price that you will pay.

From Crannóg34

Heart
Katherine Noone

Sometimes I think
you are foot steps
in the night , prompting me
to sit upright on my elbow
to listen.
It is you ticking
along on your bumpy road.

When I mourn, it is
 as if you are stilled,
weighed
down with grief.

On happy days, you leap
 at a lover's touch,
the voice of a long lost friend.

My longevity rests
with you,
as you conquer
all the valleys and peaks of life.

You were broken once.
Time
pieced you back together.

From Crannóg39

Na h-Íosadóirí
Cóilín Crua MacCraith

Itheann siad foirgnimh liath san áit seo.
Siúlann siad le meáchan na gcloch á dtarraingt siar.
Bíonn a gcuid lámha faoi ghlas slándála
agus tá cuirtíní tarraingte ar a gcuid súile.
Aréir, am éigin théis uair an mheánoíche, stop duine
acu ag siúil don chéad
uair riamh.
Sheas sé ar an imeall agus chroch a chloigeann trom i
dtreo oileáin an
chuain.
Chartaigh sé na comhaid a bhí filte go néata i
ndoimhneas a bhoilge agus
bhog sé an deasca mór adhmaid a bhí i lár pasáiste a
scornaí le
blianta.
Ansin, droim le cathrach, d'oscail sé cuirtíní na súl agus
thom é féin i
mbeatha álainn na farraige.

From Crannóg 9

53

Tradition

Aisling Keogh

I guess it's because of our history of persecution that certain traditions exist among the first peoples of Canada.

I like to think that at some point in time, these traditions served to protect our culture and our way of life. Take, for example, how tradition demands that I never speak my name to a possible enemy, well, there was a time when our people were living under such severe and constant threat, that identifying oneself would have made our small and settled community vulnerable to attack. It is because of this that, even now, when I make a new acquaintance, I must first be introduced by a friend, before I am free to offer my name.

Today I am going to break with tradition, for I do not have many friends left.

My name is Hania. It is an aboriginal name meaning "spirit warrior," and today, as I shuffle about making preparations for tonight's potlatch, I pray that I might live up to my name.

Tonight's potlatch is to be held in my honour, it is a celebration of my life. And towards tomorrows dawn there will be a ceremony during which I will give away most of my worldly possessions in preparation for the next part of my spiritual journey, for I know my time is near.

As part of these preparations I find myself wandering through the house, occasionally stopping to touch or examine different objects. It is strange to think of leaving this house, it has been my home my whole life; I was born here, and I will die here.

Soon.

But for today I need to prepare, and to consider what items I wish to bequeath to my family and friends – although the reality is that I have been pondering this for weeks now; such musings are an important part of a spiritual and emotional clearing that move me towards achieving balance between the four parts of my being, in preparation for my journey.

In recent months I have faced my trials with stoicism and resolve, so for now I will indulge myself, and other chores will have to wait.

I shuffle from room to room, gathering various objects and, when I reach the kitchen, I set them out on the table. There is a blanket for my son, my shotgun for my father, and a silver bangle for my mother.

I then play a game with myself and contemplate what I might give a wife – the wife I never had – as a token of our love down through however many years of our imagined marriage.

I glance around at the various artifacts and family heirlooms that adorn the house, many of them are quite valuable now – popular culture loves our "genuine native American antiques" – but money is not wealth, and the gift of a family heirloom would be a reminder of a culture and tradition that did not want her.

Had I married Sarah all those years ago, what could I have given her?

I met Sarah in nineteen-sixty-one. She was the one; my sun, moon and stars. A free spirit if ever there was one, Sarah came to our small settlement as a part of a delegation of government officials who wished to buy some of our land, which they needed to build a new highway. She had a degree in anthropology and a lot of principles and ideals; she was an advisor on "matters of cultural sensitivity" to this sorry delegation.

It was nineteen-sixty-one and their very presence in our small settlement was "culturally sensitive."

You see, it's a little known fact, but in 1885 the Canadian government passed a bill into law that became known as the "Potlatch Law" and it banned the practice of traditional potlatch celebrations among the indigenous tribes of North America; all in an effort to make us "civilized" and assimilate us into their mainstream culture.

As I recall it, the ban was eventually repealed in nineteen fifty-one, just ten years before I met Sarah; and while ten years might seem like a long time, as a people we had yet to forgive and forget these efforts to assimilate us and how we had been wronged. Any government official was greeted with suspicion, and was no friend of ours.

Sarah was different though, she wanted to hear our story, and in exchange for these stories she was patient, considerate, and generous with her time. Our love affair remained a secret until such time as she told me she was pregnant with my child. I wanted to marry her, but my father would not hear of it, nor would he give us his blessing.

Sarah and I planned to run away together, to go and live in the city, and live like any other young couple with a young family. We talked about it for weeks and planned our escape down to the last detail, but all the while I was struggling with the idea of disobeying my father, and with leaving behind a cultural tradition that was frail and vulnerable, and, I thought, needed its youth to protect it.

In the end it was Sarah who left me. She realised before I did that I could not, nor would I ever leave, and she slipped away during the night. Months later she got a letter to me; the letter said that she understood, and she enclosed a photograph of our son.

I reached forward and fingered the tassles on the blanket that I wish to give my son, Mitch. The blanket was made for me by my maternal grandmother at the time of my birth, and I had always wanted him to have it for his sons.

Mitch must be almost fifty years old now, and we have never met. I often wonder what I would say to him now, to explain why his father has not been a part of his life. What could I tell him? Or maybe there is no need to tell him anything at all, maybe there is some other man who has been there for him all these years; maybe there is some other man he calls Dad?

My father, Mahpee, his grandfather, also grew up without his father and it made him an angry man. Within our culture kin is so important, and my father has always been ashamed of his father's desertion.

In the absence of a father our elders embraced him as their own son and watched after him, guided him, and provided for him. He knew as much love as any other child in our small community, but his shame at his father's wrong doing was too much for one soul, and he turned this shame inwards and became angry and defensive. Mahpee was at war with the outside world.

As a child I sensed his anger, maybe I even understood it a little, because to me Mahpee was always a good father, he provided well and taught me well; his morals and values were sound.

In later years, though, I could not understand or forgive his hostility toward Sarah, or his insistence that I could not marry outside of our culture. For a week during nineteen-sixty-one he ranted and raved about the importance of our cultural tradition and the white man who had tried to destroy it. It was as though the woman I loved embodied all of the wrong doings of others; and I knew in my heart and soul that if I left with her I would not be his son, I would be the embodiment of his own father's wrong doing, and I could not do it.

In the few years after Sarah left I used look at him and wonder if tradition and honour bound him to this place in ways that did nothing to nourish his spirit or soul; I used wonder if we had more in common than either of us realised.

I reached for the gun and began to dismantle it for cleaning. The gun seems like a fitting gift for my Papa, who was angry and yet peaceable; who would use a gun only to hunt and to provide for his family. When I was very young my father taught me that if you cook a fish supper for a man who his hungry you have fed him, but if you teach that man to fish then you have fed him for life.

While I was cleaning out the barrel of the gun I found myself thinking about the relationship between my parents. They had married quite late in life, and had me even later, there are no other children in my family. I am certain that my parents loved each other, they showed it in the ways in which they honoured each other; and they complemented each other in many, many ways. But there was little joy or laughter or spontaneity in their relationship, little that I saw anyway, and I have always found it difficult to understand what might have drawn them together and made their marriage?

But what would an old man who has lived entirely alone for almost a year now know about anything?

My mother, Kaya, was a gentle soul; patient and nurturing. She taught me much about balance, and encouraged me to honour my spirits callings, even when that meant that I might leave her. To my mother I will give my silver bangle, because my love and admiration for her are eternal.

The blanket, the gun, the bangle, I leave them all in the centre of the kitchen table along with an envelope addressed to a second cousin of mine who lives in a city in B.C. Sealed inside the envelope are the deeds for this house, our land, and all of the assets of our tribe. He can do with these what he sees fit. I will leave a note with the envelope asking whoever finds the remains of my physical body to send it on to him. It is the last wish of a dying man, and I must put my faith in the kindness of a stranger to carry it through.

I must rely on the kindness of a stranger now, because there is simply nothing left of our tribe. My second cousin and his wife and children, and I, are the last inhabitants of our village, we are all that remains.

I polish the silver bangle and contemplate the notion of tradition and how powerful it is; how it gives us a sense of purpose, meaning and belonging; how it adds significance and value to the arbitrary and mundane. And how it is that when we hold onto the notion too tightly it makes us uncompromising, inflexible, antiquated and irrelevant.

For years now, there have been no marriages or births in our small community, just deaths. Our suspicion of outsiders, and our tradition of marrying within our culture, has lead to our demise.

In recent years some of our younger folk actually left our community and went to live in the surrounding cities – many without the blessings of their elders. Those of us who were left behind scathed at how the lure of the dollar had crept in to the consciousness of our young folk, and bemoaned the meaningless existence we could foresee for them. It seems to me now that they foresaw what we could not, and that they too had their own wisdom.

Ten months ago my second cousin came to me and asked for my blessing-he wished to go and begin a new life elsewhere with his family. I could not deny him that. To him I gave my blessing, and my word that I would sell whatever assets I could and use the proceeds to move to the city.

But this time I knew what Sarah had known all of those years ago, that I could not, nor will I ever leave; I am too old and too set in my ways to begin again. And so I choose to stay here alone, until death comes for me.

At about six this evening I will put the finishing touches to the feast that I have prepared, and wash and dress for the occasion. Then I will wait on the steps for no-one to arrive.

At sundown I will light a fire outside, and burn the remains of my feast so as not to attract wild animals to the house. I will make a makeshift bed on the porch, and when the sky shows the first signs of light I will lie down on the bed and pull the covers up to my chin. I will gaze at the stars while I wait for death.

First light is always a good time to begin again.

From Crannóg 29

Getting There
Kathleen O'Driscoll

Five moves in three months,
then I found my little garage flat.
It's gold dust.
Crossing to the far edges
of this madly stretched city,
I still can't buy a tin opener
in Galway.
God knows if I'll ever cook again
on a cast iron frying pan.
I forgot the old one
somewhere.
But Des Kavanagh's of Market Street
still have heaters
rather than computers
and I hope to purchase
the last mattress in town
from Tom Dempsey's of Westside
next week.
At last I've got a floor cloth
from John O'Carroll's in Salthill
and a precious packet
of cornflower seeds.

From Crannóg 8

The Dark
Stephen Shields

Call me
    two eyes that rake
    from the skies
    in the south, in the west,
    that bicker and wail

Call me
    the worm at your lip
    as you sip
    from spring water
    at the river's cradle

I am
    the palsy of men
    in barren birth tearings
    while their land
    is flayed by strife.

I am
    the caustic war frenzy
    of a hero, the din
    of his chariot
    advancing on foes

There is
    a reeling host
    scorching hills,
    brute avarice
    trailing the Dark.

From Crannóg 10

War Games

Aron Costelloe

The sky was deepest cobalt.

A noonday sun hung suspended.

Endless dunes stretched into the horizon, shimmering, as though glimpsed from behind an invisible, twitching curtain.

The sounds of the world were wind and breath and nothing else.

Dale shifted position slightly.

He opened a mouth ringed with sweat and stubble and fading acne scars and said

– Anne Boleyn had six fingers on her left hand and three nipples. If Henry's charges of Adultery and Incest had failed, he planned to use these facts to burn her as a witch.

Gorman inhaled, knuckling sweat from his left eye. – Too detailed to be anything but the truth.

– You think? countered Dale.

– Oh, absolutely. I'm surprised at you, giving yourself away so easily.

An imperceptible flicker in Dale's eyes, which nobody on earth but Gorman would have seen.

– Oh, well, now you've just sealed it, he said. – True.

– Positive?

– I'll bet next month's salary.

Dale sighed. – Pity, I could've used the money. True it is.

– Hoo hah, Gorman said, with some satisfaction.

– Would you have paid up?

– What do you think?

Sighing again, Dale lowered his binoculars. He dabbed his face with a ragged, bloodied handkerchief and said

– Faith and Belief. Multiple choice.

– Your speciality.

Gorman lapsed into a thoughtful silence, tilting his helmet a fraction. Then he said

– How many churches worldwide claim to have Christ's foreskin in their possession? Thirteen, thirty, or three hundred.

– Slippery.

– Mmmm ... hmmm.

– Common sense suggests the highest number is the correct answer, given Religion's tendency to spread everywhere and infect everything it touches.

A *slkkkkkk* noise made Dale look up. He watched a long, thin snake eddy across the sagging roof.

Gorman snorted. – My, aren't *we* feeling blasphemous today. First the Revelations-bashing at breakfast with that new cadet, now this. And you out here doing God's work and all.

– I somehow doubt this elusive God of yours would approve of *anything* we're doing out here. But if I meet him at a future date, I'll be sure to ask.

– Please do.

– I'll go with my first instinct and say three hundred.

A huge grin crept across Gorman's face. – Thirty.

Dale scowled. He picked up his canteen and poured water over his head and into his mouth.

– I see the sun is finally getting to you, Gorman remarked. – Only took a month.

– Enjoy your lead while it lasts.

– Oh, I will. And a question on Crime and Punishment, if you please. Also multiple choice.

Sensing movement, Gorman turned his head.

A fat, hairy spider was crawling along his upper thigh.

Gorman took his right hand off the stock and brushed the spider away with a grunt. It fell amongst the cauterised rubble and scuttled off.

– About time, said Dale. – I've been saving this one. Which of these activities was *not* a Hanging offence in Nineteenth century Britain: associating with gypsies, writing on Westminster Bridge, swearing in public or cutting down a tree?

Gorman licked his top lip, then his bottom lip, then his top lip.

– Every answer sounds like a contender, he conceded.

– Don't they, Dale agreed.

– Not surprised you've been saving it.

– Neither am I.

Gorman paused. Dust blew from the ledge, spiralling out of the shattered window. Straw fell from the roof.

At last he said, – It could only be the most painfully obvious option. Swearing in public.

Dale shook his head admiringly.

– Lords and New Creatures, the man hits another bullseye. If only your aim was as true.

– As I remember, it was my aim that saved you in Meymaneh.

– You can believe that if it makes you feel better. Dale raised the binoculars and leaned into the wall. – Language.

Gorman nodded silent assent.

– Language it is... which five letter word, beginning with 'U', means 'Imperial Decree', often–

– Contact, contact, Dale said hoarsely. – I repeat, *contact*. North-north- east, five hundred and twenty yards.

– Identify. Gorman clicked the safety on his weapon and pressed his eye into the sight.

– Need a second ... one second ... wait ... do you have him?

– No. No target visual.

– ... wait ... wait ... okay, got him ... it's a male, mid forties ...

– I see him, I have him. Target acquired.

– Militia head dress, Militia uniform, said Dale. – Armed with an MG4, Fort 17 pistol. Large backpack.

– I see him, I have him, I see him.

– Waiting for confirmation ... waiting ...

– He's going for cover, he's going for cover. Do I take the shot?

– Waiting to confirm ... waiting ...

– I repeat, do I take the shot?

– Go-green-go, I repeat, that's a go-green-go.

– Confirm.

– I confirm, go-green-go. Kill order, kill order, *fire fire fire.*

– Roger.

Gorman squeezed the trigger.

The rifle spat flame.

A sonic boom, caught inside the house, crackling towards the sky.

Through his binoculars, Dale saw a flash of red atop the man's head. The figure pirouetted balletically, and fell.

– Target down, said Dale. – I repeat, target down. Good job, soldier.

– We aim to please. Gorman ejected the spent round, took it, and placed it in a pocket of his fatigues. – Do you want me to repeat the question?

– No. The answer is 'Ukase.'

– 'Ukase' it is. *Very* well played.

– I agree, Dale beamed. – Well, come on, chop-chop. Time moves ever onward like the winged feet of Mercury.

– Entertainment, said Gorman.

From Crannóg 33

Sea Change
Lorna Shaughnessy

The day the tide turned at her feet
she discovered her true nature;
a mirror flashed, a silver tail flipped
and she swam into her element.

Now waves swell in her blue-green eyes,
her ear strains to catch her sisters' song,
and salt dries in the hollow prints
where she walks.

Pearls scatter in her hair, to crown
the changeling, and call to mind
an older charm, the caul that said
this child would never drown.

From Crannóg 5

Roger and Out
Sadie Murphy

Sleep now,
for in the morning,
while Roger McGough
still adorns your shelf -
now a dustman
dealing in scraps of light -
you will need
his shovel
to dig through the day.

From Crannóg 6

Diarmuid de Faoite

Never Smile at a Crocodile

He woke at six thirty, very early by his former standards. Today was Skype day, however, the day he would get to see his daughter for fifteen minutes. The electronic meeting wouldn't happen until ten but he was excited – and nervous. A wrong move on his part could lose him this weekly window of opportunity. The Sunday before last, her mother had been out so he didn't get to Skype her until twelve. A long wait at the end of a long week of waiting. When the call eventually came through, he leaped to answer it but her mother was trying to skype on her smartphone. Dropped call after dropped call, no picture, no sound. 'I'll try the girls' i-pad but it's not charged,' she texted. Eight minutes later the skype call ended as the i-pad battery died and his heart sank. He texted to suggest if she managed to charge it up she might skype back in. She didn't.

The following Sunday, he was told Tanni was sick and her mother cancelled until Wednesday. He texted on Monday to see was she any better. 'Much improved'. She attached a photo. His daughter was dressed in pale blue and white, complete with a pair of Star of David flashing antennae bobbing on a headband. She looked absolutely gorgeous in glorious sunshine. He bit his lip and deleted 'a Fenian with an Uzi: a dangerous thing,' and texted instead: 'Lovely colour in that photo, can I skype her tomorrow?' 'No it's a holiday here and we'll be out all day.' 'Enjoy the hol,' he responded and left it at that.

His mind ran amok. What kind of holiday is it? Israeli National Day? What country on earth would dress their children up like that? Then he thought of quite a few, including his own green sod, consoling himself with the thought that at least his own national day was a religious event. That notion had more holes in it than a sieve so he considered the reality of conscription instead, this time imagining his gun totting daughter giving some poor Arab a hard time at a check point. Her great granduncles had all been mad Irish Republicans who had a name for themselves by tackling Tan soldiers with their bare hands. God only knew what she might get up to in the Israeli Army with a natural inclination to fight. He recalled definitions of a legitimate target and realized his daughter was probably already one. Having fed his resentments he calmed down and went back to looking at the photo. There she was, in her youngest half-sister's arms, her eldest half-sister smiling over their shoulders at the two of them. She was dressed in pink, her sisters the ones in

blue and white and wearing the antennae. He breathed a sigh of relief and forwarded the photo on to relatives, letting them know she was doing well.

He busied himself with work then until Wednesday. By 10.25 that morning no call had come through so he started to Skype in from his end. No joy. He tried the girls' address. No joy. He texted: 'What's the story?' 'She's asleep'. He let her know he had to go out at 11.45 but would probably be back after 1.00. She responded that the afternoons tend to slip by, what with the girls and all, that she was taking her to a developmental class the following morning, so how about Friday? He let her know that a week and a half had slipped by for him without seeing his daughter and that he would really appreciate it if she could find fifteen minutes in the afternoon. She let him know in response that she had stayed in to skype that morning and if skyping was such an inconvenience for him perhaps it would be better to leave it out altogether. Soon he was dragging up her relationship with the older girls' father and she was letting him know in no uncertain terms that she would not tolerate his anger and impatience. 'Good vibes only please'. 'Good vibes beget good vibes' was his parting shot. He stayed on line for the rest of that day and most of Thursday, hoping there would be a softening. There wasn't. He went out and bought himself a smartphone then as he could no longer depend on the neighbour's Wi-Fi. He asked them in the shop to set Skype up on it. Finally, Friday came around. He showered, shaved and waited. It was time.

He crosses his fingers and texts: 'Skype?'.

'She's tired but I'll set it up now.'

Knowing the phone signal is dodgy, he runs to turn on the computer. The neighbours are away and have switched off their wi-fi. He turns to the new smart phone, says a quick prayer, more like a curse, and suddenly the screen turns pale blue as the welcoming sound of the Skype door opening sings him a welcome. He checks his contacts quickly: she's online, he can see; the girls are online too. Ok. Ok. But nothing's happening. He calls her. No answer. He calls the girls. No answer. He puts on the kettle. Tries again. Still nothing.

Texts: 'On line now'. Nothing. Kettle boils, teabag in cup, starts to pour. Incoming Skype call! Scalds himself. 'Aww Fuck, fuck, fuck!' Grabs the phone in one hand, turns the cold tap on with the other, terrified he'll hit the wrong button or knock it off somehow or let it fall into the sink. The screen is screaming at him that 'the girls' are calling; they have put up a lovely photo of an orchid as their tag. He attempts the art of swiping to take the call, his fingers gliding across the screen. It continues to ring. It will ring out soon. He swipes again. No go. Then he notices one doesn't swipe to receive Skype calls one hits the green button. He hits it. It still rings. This new technology bamboozles him. He checks his finger tip to see if it's hot or cold and decides he needs to leave it on the green button a bit longer. He does. Nothing. Still ringing. He starts tapping the screen like mad. The ringing stops. His heart is swallowed down the plughole of Skype's 'no answer' tone. Call ended. Silence.

Texts begin to fly, the tension in the wording already beginning to ratchet up. He tries ringing her but doesn't get through. His hand throbs from the burn so he goes back to the still running tap and overflowing sink for some cold water comfort. He plunges his hand into the sink displacing water onto the floor and sighs for his loss and his wet shirt, feeling tears of anger and despair well up into his eyes. The phone rings, its making the Skype tone again. This time he gets to turn the tap off, grab a tea towel and study the screen. It's the girls again. The screen gives him three options, a red button to end the call – don't hit that one - a green one to take the call and another one that says video call. He wonders what he did wrong the last time and presses the video button. No response. Tries the other green button. No response. He is about to throw his new smartphone against the blank wall in front of him when the touch screen responds and he hears her mother whine a melancholic 'hiii'. She's an Eastern European Jew. He checks himself as he realizes he now hates her voice and is quickly becoming a racist. He also knows he's the melancholic one and has promised to be positive. He puts on his best smiley face, switches to video call which works seamlessly this time, his face appearing in a small square in the bottom right hand corner of the screen. The rest of the screen is black, however. 'Can you see me?' 'Yes'. 'I can't see ...' then the screen becomes a blur, sees her mother's brown hair, catches a bit of her nose, there's a hint of pink, the woollen cardigan she loves to wear and looks so beautifully feminine in, the sound of movement, another pair of hands, an exterior sliding door opens and there she is on a patio, Tanni, dressed all in white with tiny little teddy bear ears peeking out of the top of the hood of her baby gro.

Why is she hooded up like that? Is she not too hot? He is about to say something when a hand swiftly removes the hood and he gets to see Tanni's head in all its beautiful bald glory. Her eyes are almost black. He swims in them. He is fascinated by her eyes. He speaks and she seems to turn to the screen in recognition. He speaks more, desperate for her to recognize him. She seems curious, concerned even. She starts to cry. Instinctively, he starts to sing. He sings the song he sang for her in the womb. She settles. She says 'Ah!'. He says 'Ah!' Tanni looks astounded and says 'Ah!' again. He says 'Ah!' in response, even louder than before. She gives another 'Ah' and he tops her with a really big, loud one. It doesn't have the desired effect and she goes quiet. He kicks himself for trying to outdo his baby in an 'Ah!' competition and goes back to singing.

Her eldest sister's pony-tail falls into the frame from time to time. She has been instructed not to engage with him so the only sound, apart from the baby's 'ah', is the hum of traffic in the background. The sky is a blue he hasn't seen in years. Tanni lies on a thick green foam play mat on wooden decking in the shade, the white baby gro enhancing her olive brown skin. 'It must be so warm there,' he blurts, convinced she must be roasting. He repeats the comment. Tanni's eldest sister monotones uneasily 'It's not... she's not too hot' and says no more. A burgundy creeper in full bloom curls up one of the posts behind her and above and beyond that a palm tree sways in the breeze. Tanni suddenly flips onto her belly, 'I can't see her!' he cries, almost panic stricken. Her sister moves to reposition the i-pad, revealing a magnolia coloured, five story apartment block above them and a cloudless sky. The panoramic sweep crashes back down to earth and the screen goes black all of a sudden. Did it fall on the baby? He hears a 'sorry' and after a moment the screen becomes an orange blur then becomes a blur of white and brown, steadies and focuses. He sighs and tries to make light of it: 'Phew! That was close!' Tanni turns towards the sound. She reaches out to touch, as if trying to touch the screen, to touch him, perhaps. 'Yes, darling, its me, Daddy! Abba!' He sings for her once more as she continues to grab at the screen, driven by recognition. She lunges again and he laughs, 'Yes, darling, oh I can't wait to see you,'. Once more she reaches and a multi-coloured, caterpillar-like soft toy appears with a green, smiling, gaping, crocodile head. As Tanni hauls it in, her balance shifts and she is on her back again, wrestling the elongated creature that's as long as she is with all her limbs while chewing determinedly on its right ear. She turns and the head of the toy completely obliterates his view of Tanni but affords him a close up of a crocopillar's smile.

He goes quiet, hates the toy and then starts an even more determined singing. He tries to remember the polka she liked but it eludes him. 'Hup Hup, horsey!' seems to elucidate a response so he repeats that one though he thinks its crap and wants her to have a proper musical education. Suddenly, she turns to the screen and gives a huge smile, her black eyes dancing in her head. He nearly swoons. 'Hello my little darling, hello my love,' he coos. 'Yes, its Daddy!' He brings his face to the screen and gives it two big kisses. When he pulls back he sees she is on her belly once more, drooling, head up, legs kicking and chanting 'ahh ya ya'. He joins in, careful not to outdo her this time. She responds. She responds again! But now her legs are kicking furiously and she begins to complain and cry. She wants to be picked up. Her mother's voice is heard. 'Have to go now.' He knows its been only seven minutes and he starts to sing to her, trying to calm her. She wants up. 'She's upset, we have to go.' He tries singing again. The baby wants up. 'It's no good, you must go.' Reluctantly, he says his goodbyes, 'Bye, Tanni, see you again soon, bye!' He gets a 'bye' in return, unsure as to who mouthes it and all contact is smothered by the end of call tone. Call with Prescilla ended, 10.13. He decides there and then he will ask for a second weekly skype session and books a flight to Israel.

In a satellite suburb of Tel Aviv, a woman tells her daughter to turn off the i-pad and pick up the baby. 'We'll be going to the beach soon,' she tells them in English, 'I have the bags ready.' A breeze rustles the palm fronds and plays with the end of her light skirt as she returns into the cool, white interior of her apartment. In the bedroom she lies down and tries to breathe steadily once more. Just breathe. Breathe as she recalls the screaming, as she recalls the window being smashed, the baby on the floor between them, her having refused to turn down the heat. She remembers the breach delivery, the seemingly dead baby, the brain damage, the cooling therapy, Tanni's miraculous recovery and their flight into Israel. She sees his beautiful smile, the glint in his eye and promises herself never again. A text comes through. 'She looks great. I'll be over at Easter.' She makes a call. That evening, while her mother minds the children, she changes her will.

From Crannóg 36

Fossils on Feathers

Chloe Diskin

If and when you die one day,
You never really go away
And I don't mean afterlife (what's with that anyway?)
I mean what I say.

Hundreds and thousands ... and millions!
Of years

From now my dears
Your bones will be recovered from the rocks
Or the sand of a box

And people will look at them
And try to know exactly when
You were born and bred and daily fed
And they'll see a pile of leaves and think it was your bed!

But you the ball of crystal
And eyes like dying embers,
Will chant and scream and shout like crazy,
Saying no no! ha ha! You've got it all
So very wrong!
In my day we slept upon
Mattresses of feathers

From Crannóg 2

Perfection

Hanahazukashi

Eager to calculate my points I skid over to Mama and ask to borrow the pen she keeps in her purse. Back in my seat I start reading the questions, hurriedly wanting to check off the ones that talk about me and add up my points.

Not yet, no, not yet. My eyes are quickly scanning and finding nothing. Aha! 'Moving Family Homes.' That's a whopping 300 points! But then I read the words in parenthesis: (within the last three years). Darn. We moved six years ago, and I can't really remember Ohio at all. I wonder if I could give myself 100 points.

'Arrival of A Younger Sibling.' I miss that one by a few years, too.

I finally get a few points toward the bottom for 'Returning from A Vacation' and 'Finishing the School Year and Moving Up A Grade.' A measly 30 points. I wanted to do a lot more adding. Some of them give 500 points. 'Divorce of Parents.'

I look over at Mama sitting on the ground of the doctor's waiting room, playing with Eduardo. He is pushing a wooden ball up and around circling wire. Then my mother follows with a green ball, chasing Eduardo around the 3D maze.

'Mama?'

'Yes, Bala?'

I run to her and show her the magazine. 'Mama, I hardly got any points.'

'What is it?' She looks over as she puts her arm around Eduardo, to make sure he doesn't wander off while she's not looking.

'This. You get points for the things that happen in your life.'

'Honey, this is for stress. It's good if you don't have a lot of points.'

'Do you think I can get points for moving from Ohio to McAllen? I know it was six years ago and the magazine says three, but can I still count it?'

'Bala, it's for parents worried about their kids. You don't have to take this. It's for kids who have trouble at home or at school.'

'Like if kids don't get on the Honor Roll?'

'Mhm, or maybe their father dies. Or their parents get a divorce.' I try to think of someone I can tell to take the test, but no one comes to mind. Everyone at school is fine. I think about the kids in books and movies wearing torn jeans or caps on backward. Do those kids really exist anywhere? If they do, are their parents taking this test?

'Eduardo Cepeda!'

In the doctor's office, after my brother's turn,

I sit on the plastic paper and stare at my knees, wondering how they know to send my legs forward when Dr. Gomez taps them with the rubber triangle. What would happen if my leg didn't move? What would it mean? I decide to not let my left leg fly and will it to stay still with my tensed jaw.

I stare. Out it flies. Rats.

We have a snack after we pick up Iko and arrive home. Opening three napkins, Mama places apple pieces, two cookies, and raisins and peanuts in three of the four squares. I pour myself a class of orange juice and place it in my fourth square.

We go outside, bike our standard ten laps around the neighborhood, and then get to play a game of basketball. I shower, read, kiss my father mandatorily when he arrives homes and set the table for dinner. A few hours later, 'Goodnight, Bala. I love you.' and the door fits into its frame.

I am alone in my room with Pink Bear, God, and dark blue curtains letting in ripples from the universe as the wind breathes. It's the rarest of days, when we can have open windows, the cold front of sixty degrees letting us turn off the air conditioner for the night.

My lack of points from the magazine fizzles up my legs, through my stomach and up into my chest. 'Everything is too simple', the tingle mocks, the tiniest of nags, asking me about how and why I am living.

I hush it, the devil, the unclean. I kick down the comforter and kneel at the bottom of the bed, close my eyes, and prepare to open them and register the first star I see. If I make a wish upon the wrong star, my wish won't be granted, or worse, the opposite might occur.

Go!

Open and the star to the right is the brightest and I utter my wish and prayer, all desires and dreams wrapped up in God. 'Please help me be with you in heaven, Lord. Please help me go to heaven. I love you so much. Please let everything be okay. I will do what you say.'

I blink three times, visualize God in his big arm chair, and kiss heaven, to make sure He's heard me. After the nightly ritual is finished, my eyes anxiously move from star to star, trying to really feel God and His home. I imagine my body rising closer to the dome of black and can feel the stars stretching out in a huge embrace around Robin Avenue and my family. There is robust, meticulous love. Storytime, Our Father, Hail Mary, Glory Be, Now I Lay Me, Prayers for Family, Goodnight Song, Drink of Water in the Yellow Cup, One Minute Snuggling Time, and 'Goodnight. I love you.' The love is unmistakable, kneaded into each child since we were born to the family, the loyalty there without deciding, method unquestioned: traditional, logical, right.

Suddenly, I feel myself parting from my parents and Iko downstairs, from Eduardo next door, being pulled toward sky and future and God more powerfully than ever before. I feel God telling me I am completely separate from everyone on Earth, and tied only to Him and His will. The tingle comes again, this time with excitement. Eyes closed in benediction, deep breaths and the vow 'I will do everything for you. I love you.'

After several minutes, I lie back down and can't stop smiling, the breeze and the dancing curtain so exciting to my South Texan skin.

From Crannóg 48

Na Crainnte

Máire iníon Bhreathnaigh

I gcoillín úr
i measc na ndriseóg
bhí dhá fhearnóg ag fás.

San Earrach, tháinic an méid sin spreagadh
i bhfás na nduilleóg
go raibh dídean acu
in aghaidh ceathanna an t-Samhraidh

Chómh brioghmhar is a bhi siad!

Leag siad a fhallaing duilleach ar an talamh
i ndeire an Fhomhair,
agus shín siad amach
le na sgith a leigint
i rith an Gheimhridh.

Tréimhse roimh Nollaig
Bhí toirneach agus tinntreach ann.
Sgriosadh crann amhain.

Tá an ceann eile in a sheasamh
i lom agus tanai
ag brathnú i gcómhnuí
ar an cheann atá sgriosta.

From Crannóg 7

Perfect Day

Caroline Nolan

We could spend all day,
you and I
in the little pub on the corner;
feigning intelligence,
simulating sex appeal,

squeezing new inspiration
from the already starved air,
so we may clog the world
with (yet more) cryptic poetry,

sinking pints of the black stuff
drawn by American high school graduates
who sleep with our men -
for six months. And later,

when our egos have been sated,
by the merry pounding
of each other's flesh,

we could write
about our perfect day.

From Crannóg 3

This Guessing Game
Margaret Faherty

'In London for a holiday?' The voice was thin and nervous. Claire nodded and smiled at the woman squeezing herself into the seat beside her.

'Flying frightens the daylights out of me. This is my second time up and my last. Will you give me a hand with this please?' The woman was struggling unsuccessfully with her seatbelt. Blobs of sweat dotted her upper lip. The belt pressed tightly on her large wobbly stomach.

'Thank you. I'll be glad to get home I can tell you. A whole month I've been away; staying in Ruislip with my daughter I was. Yes, I was looking after my grandchildren. Mary, that's my daughter, had her varicose veins done. You wouldn't believe the size of her ulcers. Like rotten tomatoes. I had my hands full. England's no place to rear children.'

Claire felt she had to say something. As the plane took off, her neighbour blessed herself and began to finger her rosary beads. Soon they were flying over a duvet of soft white clouds you'd like to wrap all around you. She'd been surprised by the mauve duvets, frilly pillow cases and pastel-coloured walls in the clinic instead of the starched white sheets and hospital green walls she'd expected.

'What would you like to drink?'

The woman stopped fingering the beads to answer the stewardess. 'A cup of tea please.'

'I'll have a vodka and tomato juice please. A Bloody Mary!'

Her neighbour made loud sucking noises as she drank her tea. She pointed to Claire's glass. 'I don't know how you drink that stuff'.

She didn't answer.

'From Dublin yourself?'

Claire nodded. Surely the woman would get the message and leave her alone.

'I guessed as much. Dublin girls are more stylish than country girls. I'm from County Limerick. Staying in London with friends, were you?'

'I was.' Shelia had proved to be a real friend. Without question or comment, she'd arranged for Claire to be admitted to a clinic, a large converted Victorian house with evergreens in its back garden just off Finchley Road. They'd had tea in 'Louis's' just before Shelia had dropped her off. The pianist had played 'Moonlight and Roses,' a background to the chatter of hennaed ladies stuffing themselves with Louis' famous meringues. Next day when she woke from the anaesthetic, the tune had continued to play in her head and there had been a taste of meringue in her mouth.

There had been very little blood.

'Think of it as nothing more than a simple D and C,' John had smilingly urged. Neither had there been post-anaesthetic blues or a feeling of guilt. She congratulated herself on her practical non-emotional approach to the whole business. John would be pleased. 'Good girl,' he'd smile. 'That's my Claire.'

Could he really not have managed to join her in London for a day? The day she'd got out of the clinic perhaps? He had travelled over and back often enough on business. 'No place, England, for Irish people to live.' Again the accusing voice assaulted her. 'It breaks my heart to see my grandchildren growing up there. Little pagans they are.' It didn't seem to matter if Claire answered or not.

'The dirt those children are allowed to watch on television.' She paused to suck in her breath. 'Of course, I jumped up and switched off the television.' It was difficult to imagine the woman jumping up. Claire laughed. Shelia had managed to make her laugh the night she had come out of the clinic. After a few glasses of wine, instead of feeling sad or maudlin, Claire went to bed laughing.

Gin, coupled with the fact that John was back after a month's absence, had made her careless. She'd first met him at one of Jane's parties, stilted affairs where you stood around slowly sipping Muscadet. When she'd noticed him, John had been standing by the window looking bored. Afterwards she realized that his expression came not from boredom but from the way he lifted his eyebrows.. 'You're not married I see.' The woman was looking at Claire's left hand. You're better off the way marriages are going nowadays. Still despite everything, I suppose children and grandchildren make up for the rest of it.' She sniffed and licked chocolate embedded in the folds of her mouth.

John's marriage and his separation had been as civilised as was everything about him. Incompatible after the first few years, he and his wife had decided to stay married until the children had finished school. Often, after he and Claire has been in the company of married couples, he'd put his arm around her and say, 'relationships like ours are so much better than marriage, don't you think?'

A four-bedded room in the clinic was the best Shelia had been able to manage at short notice. When Claire hadn't been able to stop herself from saying, 'I hate sharing,' Sheila had laughed. 'You're all in for the same thing. In Russia they do it during the lunch hour in something like a dentist's chair.' In the clinic, she'd worn an old slightly faded nightie, a high-necked Victorian garment. Two of the other women in the four-bedded room had worn flimsy new-looking nighties like they were bought especially for the occasion. Jenny, a Yorkshire girl, occupying the bed beside Claire, had worn a red night shirt with a picture of a teddy bear.

Jenny didn't talk. The other two women had chatted with the kind of desperate chatter Claire associated with a doctor's waiting room. When Jenny had woken from the anaesthetic, she and Claire had been alone in the ward. The sound of the girl's crying had brought Claire to sit by her bed and hold her hand. In a voice bordering on hysteria, she confided in Claire. 'We tried so hard to have a baby.' The Yorkshire accent was difficult to understand. 'I went to Greece with my sister four months ago. It was the only time in my life I did it with anyone else.' A harsh laugh cut through her sobbing. 'Ouzo and the sun. And he was black.' She looked pleadingly at Claire. 'I couldn't have taken the chance, could I?'

Tonight Claire and John would talk the whole thing through. John was such a logical clear-headed person. The night she'd told him, she'd had a faint hope, a glimmer really, that he'd say, not immediately, he never spoke impulsively on important matters but afterwards: 'Claire, I've been thinking. Let's keep the baby.' Sarah and Paul were the names she'd always wanted when she'd thought of children, of their children. God, it was all so difficult when you gave it a name. 'Stop it Claire.'

The woman was leaning towards her. 'I wish that daughter of mine would come home and put some rearing on those poor children. Despite their queer accents, I'd love to have them with me.'

Claire smiled. 'I'm too old by far, Claire,' he'd said the night she'd told him. 'I've reared my children. And you're getting on too. Think of what a baby would do to our lives.'

He was right of course. He a father again at 49 and she a first time mother at 33. Wasn't their relationship the envy of their friends? No strings, companionship, sex, cosy dinners at home, good restaurants, non-package holidays, interests shared. Her apartment the perfect love nest, his mews an oasis of peace in Dublin 4. Cocoons to cosset their love.

'Ladies and Gentlemen, please fasten your seat belts.'

'Have a toffee dear. My daughter told me it was good to suck a sweet when the plane was going down.'

Claire helped the woman carry her brown paper parcels to the baggage reclaim room. After she'd watched the woman's attempts at lifting her case off the conveyer belt, Claire got a trolley for both of them. Together, they walked towards the green light. 'Thanks for helping me dear. You've only a little bag yourself.'

Claire smiled. 'I always travel light.'

'A woman who's let her figure go looks unattractive even in designer clothes,' John would comment when one of their friends had put on weight. Carefully casual in his sheepskin and Burberry scarf, he stood out from the waiting crowd. She'd never looked at him with critical appraisal before.

'Is someone meeting you dear?'

'Yes.'

Could she suggest to John that they take this dumpy woman to the train station? She wasn't sure.

'Welcome home darling.' Kissing her, he looked enquiringly at her companion.

'Will you take this lady to the bus, John?'

'Of course'. Smiling he took the trolley and pushed it towards the waiting bus. She looked at the woman awkwardly heaving herself on to the bus, her ill-fitting coat stretched tight over her fat body.

When he came back, he kissed her again. 'You look tired darling'

'I am a bit. That woman didn't help, ear-bashing me all the way from London.'

He squeezed her arm. 'You should have ignored her.'

'She wasn't a bad sort in her own way I suppose.' Claire wondered why she was defending the intrusive country woman. Why was she annoyed she hadn't suggested they drive her to the train station.

John had organised a coming-home dinner. He was the only person she knew who could manage to get a take-away from one of Dublin's exclusive restaurants. She watched him open a bottle of champagne they only drank on special occasions.

Claire didn't eat much and afterwards she knew the wine had gone to her head. He didn't comment as she told him about the clinic with the evergreen in its garden. Every now and then he stroked her hair almost mechanically.

'We'll put it out of our heads now, Claire. It's better for us to forget the whole thing. After tonight, we won't discuss it again.'

As she listened to him plan a weekend at their favourite hotel in Connemara, sudden tears streamed down her face.

'You're overtired Claire. I've got something from my GP to help you sleep.'

'Thanks John. That was thoughtful of you.'

In the bedroom he stood with her before the mirror. 'Look at yourself! You're worn out.'

He'd never seen her like this before. John took such childish pleasure in looking over her shoulder as she checked her makeup or adjusted her dress. Would he have continued to indulge this pleasure if her stomach had become large and her ankles swollen.

Better to stop this guessing game.

From Crannóg 1

Stormy Night
Billy Murray

Avoided for a while
then full on it comes
a wave full on in the chest,
dancing eyes, giddy tones
of form, salivating mood
wanting something else,
desire ...

The want to escape
a habit of a lifetime,
running from reflections
that hide behind black
silhouettes of multiple
lampposts
along an endless street,
joined at the hip
by white lines
right up the middle
of the wet macadam,
neon light splashing
on the dark night ...

when I am old I'll be famous and beautiful
and handsome and rich
and happily married,
so I will.

you hoo hoo
I wanna be like you hoo hoo
talk like you, walk like you.

screaming, looking for the party,
the action that takes
you out.
Bliss, part of the universe,
fitting in, just fix me, give it to me
that piece of the jigsaw that lets me be.

From Crannóg 7

Laughter Lines
Noelle Lynskey

To truly laugh, you must be able to take your pain and play with it!
Charlie Chaplin

I would if I could
skydive through
the watery loneliness
of your brown eyes,
salvaging you from
the anchor of anguish
dragging you down.

I would if I could
swing from the rafters,
veering your gaze skyward
reviving the ring
of your laughter,
lost in the loss of love.

I would if I could
leap through hoops of fire,
rekindling that vital
spark in your soul,
inspiring that zest for fun,
she liked best in you.

I would if I could
breathtakingly fly
on a high trapeze,
alighting
softly,
on your leaking heart
squeezing gently to heat.

I would if I could
return you to the ring once more,

master of your destiny,
laughter lilting a loud homecoming,
your clowns, drowned in mourning,
allowed once more the freedom of your eyes,
your thinned face now graced with roguish grins
as you juggle your pain in bubbles of memory.

She would,
if she could;

If I could,
I would.

From Crannóg 10

The Idea of You

Blue Germein

Is it the idea of you
that makes me feel this way
would the reality
melt my care away

I've often imagined how it would feel
wrapped up inside your arms
but you are not free to start loving me
I must resist your charms

Is it the idea of you ...

It cost me a lot to say go to you
when I hungered for your caress
it cost me a lot to say no to you
when my heart was saying yes

Is it the idea of you ...

So I'll go on keeping my heart from you
protecting myself from pain
I will not let love's magic start with you
but still these thoughts remain
Is it the idea of you ...

From Crannóg 3

Wave

Connie Masterson

Dressed in layers
of silk scarves
you dance
arms outstretched
with wings of coloured silk
that quiver like fins -
the kitchen, suddenly,
transformed into
an exotic aquarium;
entranced, we follow
your flitting performance.

And perhaps,
on the eve of the Epiphany,
a visit from one of the three
bearing golden moments,
pure essence
or mermaid's mirror.

While the natural world brings
its tidal wave of sorrow, joy
breaks through with your
splendid Angel Fish dance.

From Crannóg 9

The Reclaim

Catherine Heaney

Hurricane winds drive waves up the street
To crash on first floor walls of offices and restaurants,
Disappearing behind gaping windows,
The shutters half unhinged
Clattering to the frantic rhythm of the flood.

No voice ghosts from these interiors,
No movement glimpsed in shafts of light that
Dart from off the water,
Only shadows,
Deep like mud and thick with tragic secrets.

Suddenly, haughty, confident and black,
A wild pig pokes his head out from the darkness,
Snout twitching, sniffs,
Seems to approve,
Then with a dainty move slips into the water
And proprietorially swims down the street.

From Crannóg 10

Curriculum Vitae
Margaret Maguire

1965
stratford-on-avon.
miss bullock and the stuffed cats on the landing so
dark,
so tired.
henry the fourth part two
she's turned the pram over again nice neighbours,
he's back from hospital – learns to walk again.
you won it, wore it, kept it, gave it me.
me on daddy's shoulders in harcourt st big coat that
was funny.
the trees are in their autumn beauty
peter shaefer - royal hunt of the sun - that wonderful
cloak I made
the light is dimmer
so tired
first prize at the flower power party
my first steps miraculous photo.
poor sylvia plath
dad I've got a degree
first communion all so white fresh flowers the smell
white socks too so pure.
the heart is a lonely hunter poor ted hughes
killiney beach sour salty smell stones huge waves sand
in the jam sandwiches hold my hand don't be afraid
we'll jump in together
hold on tight maria!
he doesn't love me anymore
the agony

the day you were born the ecstasy.
rain it must be evening.
the hospice
I love you mother Baggot St. Hospital Dad 82
i love you father
1982
spain buzzing of heat paella scarlet flowers so brown
shiny
felt beautiful

1969 – inish mean honeymoon landed on the moon
oh rose thou art sick
new york smell of food everywhere noise scott
fitzgerald
killiney wild garlic crushed underfoot,
i love you
graham greene the end of the affair banned so silly
the famous five
the chalet school & jo.
little women oh beth
its getting darker
so tired
oh joy that in our embers is something that doth live
the dubliners in tallaght dancing with luke kelly
if you feel like singing do sing an Irish song
he pushed you in he didn't know you could have
drowned,
bright shards of water in that white heat
i wish they'd turn the lights on.

From Crannóg 6

Searching for Yolanda

Patrick Hewitt

Your message (furtive was it not?) was received by me in Dublin last Thursday evening. Delightfully *raffinement* as it might be described In the 75th arrondisment Of Paris, and very much to the liking of a man searching pour *complicite de corps et d'esprit.*

For some reason,which is not biblical,but perhaps has something to do with a recent fleeting encounter, I want to call you Martha. But the 'feisty bird' whom you describe yourself as suggests to me that you might reject such a name. May I, for the time being, call you Yolanda?

Let me tell you about an experience in a Mediterranean city. It was just a couple of weeks ago in a restaurant near the Placa Reial in Barcelona.

The woman sitting a few tables away in the restaurant in the Carrer Vidra is burning. Her hair is a tangled organised head of flames, a crimson yellow. Her cheeks are glowing like embers in a furnace. Her cool pink blouse envelops her burning bosom, but without conflagration. It is Exodus again, Yolanda, "the bush burned with fire, and the bush was not consumed.'

Occasionally, I catch her eyes which are a sea of flame and interest. As her back undulates, a gap emerges between the bottom of her blouse and the top of her dark jeans allowing knowledge of her body. She is forever moving in her chair, conversing energetically with her friend.

She is burning. Although I cannot see her nipples, I know that they are two red-hot cinders. Her breasts are full in the two loose cups in her blouse, which is stretched tight across her back.

Sitting with her is a slightly older woman. Her hair is short and black, with just occasional streaks of grey. She wears glasses with thin metal frames, and is dressed in a silk work shirt, and gives the sense that she is familiar with the cultivation and harvesting of chestnuts and figs and olives. She is relaxed, and, smiling easily, gives complete witness to the incandescence at the table.

They are sharing a large jug of sangria, that sweetened drink of red wine with fruit, named from a word in the Spanish so suggestive of blood. There are some plates of tapas on the table. I cannot keep my eyes from her. I feel the flood of the sublime light which she is shedding. I bathe in it.

By what laws does this young woman live, what laws sustain her? What laws, I want to ask you Yolanda, sustain the soul that inhabits her body?

When she gets up to leave the restaurant I notice a ring on her fourth left-hand finger. Somebody has married her. I watch her as she disappears into the half-light of the city square, a pulsar through the night, sending out regular bursts of sexual energy, a sensual supercharged aura. Where and how does she sleep, Yolanda?

The following day I am at the Estacio de Sants railway station for a short journey up the coast to Mataro. A woman gets on the train. She is weeping uncontrollably. She rushes to a vacant seat. Sitting by the window she covers her face with her hand, and leans her head against the window pane. Her face is almost invisible, covered by her jet black hair. It is a Monday morning in July in Barcelona. Her chest is heaving heavily. She is a heavily tanned woman, Yolanda, in her early forties I would say. In one hand she holds her train ticket. She carries no luggage. She is trying to reconcile herself. I see the pain of some terrible loss.

She succeeds in regaining a little composure, and permits herself some glances around the carriage, her eyes forlorn, long vistas of desolation.

Just then two musicians, a cellist and a banjo-player, join the crowded train. They play a version of the Beatles tune *Those were the days.* At this the woman breaks down again, and goes into a deep sobbing.

The two musicians, unaware of the woman, drive the tune harder and harder, speeding up their playing into a frenzy. The woman is in pieces, and is distraught.

She again covers her face with her hand, and seeks deeper protection in the corner between the back of her carriage seat and the windowpane.

Having completed their tune, the musicians collect money from the passengers, before disembarking at the next stop   The woman succeeds in controlling herself for a second time, and then appears to drift into a sleep of repose. She is wearing a blouse with bright colours, blues and yellows and white. One can see her in the Mango department store on the day she bought this garment, confident and poised as she regards herself in the shop mirror, anticipating the kind of days which these delighted colours suggest. For sure, Yolanda, she did not buy this blouse in tears, nor did she buy it to shed tears in. Now the colours are saturated in grief.

For this morning she has clearly suffered grievously, and there is nothing she can do. The rending sadness of life is visible.

Out in the country again, the carriage is lit up

by strong sunlight, the violent light of Spain as Hemingway has described it. The woman again lifts her head, and looks around. On her alluvial face there are dried up streams. Her eyes are two ponds on a grey day in late autumn.

It is still only July, but the year is already beginning to take its toll. Last night as I sat in an open-air restaurant one leaf and then another drifted onto my table. Yolanda, I read your message on Thursday night. With the words 'clandestine assignations are all dangerous but often very rewarding,' you have distilled a potion. Your words are a fertile rain. I can sense again the Februarys of my youth.

I look out the hotel window. The city is once again a gallery, a vista of expectancy.

You remember a week last Friday morning, Yolanda, when that completely blue sky we had been waiting for all summer finally arrived. As I walk from Merrion Square to an office In Lower Leeson Street, I become aware that a Barcelona blue has enveloped the streets and the buildings. Somewhere along Fitzwilliam street a tall young woman emerges from an office some 100 paces away, and walks on ahead of me, black Spanish hair, white blouse, and black jeans, her hips moving in harmony with the perfect day, you know that reciprocating motion, Yolanda, a suggestion of considerable amplitude; an amplitude of form and structure, answering to the mind, as Lamb put It.

Those rear cheeks are a full cargo, a cargo laden with treasure of great value, with goods of an extremely delicate nature.

There is a sense of nobleness about her, reminding me how the poet in his ballad *The Spanish Lady* felt that in all his life he 'ne'er did see a maid so sweet about the soul.'

Her hips oscillate, a plumb line, defining an exquisite rhythmical movement of perfect measure and proportion. I breathe emancipation.

Remaining overnight in the Hotel St. George, I go to bed with an issue of *Le Monde des Livres*. The photograph on the first page captivates me. It is a black and white study of the writer Lydie Salvayre. The way she reveals her thighs interests me deeply. But it is her face which gives all the interest to her thighs. Otherwise, they could be the legs of any model, of any pop-star.

The dress is also excellent. You will agree when you see it? But it is her face which says everything. There are complete mysteries to be explored in her thighs. And her face says this, tells you this without any doubt.

Her face suggests many sensual things but I imagine that these sensual mysteries are only available to a very few … the specially chosen. A man might place his hand between her thighs a thousand times and he will always learn new things. Her mystery is inexhaustible. I am sure of it.

Below the photograph is a caption which proposes that 'engagement and subversion' is suggested. Engagement and subversion: yes Yolanda, it is this and other things which I need to experience with a woman.

Tell me Yolanda: are you a woman who likes to write, who needs to express herself in words - written words? Are you driven, driven by a compulsion to snatch some thing desperately fleeting, and capture it on a page.

Are you married, Yolanda. And if you are, do you feel that there are sexual experiences which you have never had. Do you have a tight behind, with curves which wonderfully fill a tight black trousers, like waitresses who work in fashionable Italian restaurants, whose black hair IS resonant of black Italian grapes.

Is your tight behind matched by a severe face, and do you wear glasses which suggest that you look at the world In a way which expects the highest standards in art, in work, and in sophistication.

Do you wear a mid-riff length leather jacket and blue denim jeans which … well, yes, are in excruciating harmony with those immaculate tight curves of your rear.

Do you sit alone in restaurants and read Proust and Kundera and Antunes?

Are you in pain? Are you pained sometimes by the lack around you of an understanding of the breathlessly crushingly sensual nature of the world?

Do you like the sun? Have you lain on a Spanish beach wearing only a thong which was almost invisible, yet your severe face gave mystery to everything, covered you, accentuating and heightening the sense of your womanhood.

Tell me about yourself, Yolanda. I am searching everywhere for you. Of course, I have seen you many times, but always at the other side of the street, or a few seats away from me in the theatre. Now that you are at last reading this mess

From Crannóg 10

Beithigh
Piaras Ó Droighneáin

Amuigh a bhíodar
Ar an tsráid,
Mór agus aisteach
Éalaithe as garraí thuas,
Droch-chlaí,
Bogtha ag adharca
Agus pusanna fliucha,
Iad imníoch anois
Ní thuigeann siad an tsaoirse nua seo,
'Chaon bhúir acu,
Macalla láidir ag baint creatha
As tost na maidine,
Faitíos le brath sna súile móra uisciúla,
An bhfuil aon mheabhair iontu
Nó an bhfuil ann ach dorchadas ag síneadh siar.

Feiceann said thú go tobainn
Geit bainte astu ar feadh nóiméad,
Seasann said talamh,
Ach ansin drible san aer
Imíonn leo go humhal
Cloigne móra cromtha,
Suas arís an bóthairín beag,
Ach breathnaíonn ceann siar
Ag caitheamh súil cham ort,
Ag faire an laoi lena taobh,

An bhfuil said ag cuimhniú anocht ar an eachtra
Mar a chuimhníonn tusa anois
Ag féachaint ar lorg na gcrúba sa talamh,
Oscailtí dhorcha rounáilte fós le feiceáil
Faoi sholas Gealaí.

From Crannóg 37

Cáirde Ozone
Máire Uí Eidhin

Nach paiteanta an mhaise dhuit
Ar ancaire i mbarr sceiche,
Do chlann 's céile nide
Go clúmhar gárdáilte
Fíor árd os cionn fuinneoga
Mo leithide, fós go ciúin
Faoi shuan taobh thiar
Do chomhlaí dorcha.

Binneas dod' chluas
Cór na n-éan sa maidhneachan
A gcomhcheol, siosarnach duilleoga.
Cloiseann tú ceol na fuiseoige
I do cheann dhá huireasa,
Fós drúcht na maidine,
Ag slíocadh do mhín chlúimh shíoda
Mar shlinneán na bplásóg deá phioctha.

Cóta ar do dhroim níor fáisceadh ort,
Sparán, níl i do phóca thíos
Siopa riamh níorbh fheasach duit,
Bia úr ar ball
Gan bord dáileóidh tú,
Is nach beag damáiste
Don "ozone" thuas go deo
Ní dhéanfaidh tú.

From Crannóg 18

Separation
Mary O'Malley

No. Love should not end like this.
A box of tissues, a dotted page.
'Sorry. Everyone finds it hard.
Sign here.' The back of our marriage
Certificate is white. On my left hand
The gold mark of your absent wedding band
Comes up like invisible ink as I unwrite
My name, reversing the vow. Shame rises
In a tidal blackout. X is innocent. Cunning
Life has us outfoxed. I sign the forms
Consenting to our surgical untwinning.
In another room you are doing the same.

With a cheap pen, across a scratched desk.
Where is the photographer, the ridiculous cake?

From Crannóg 9

Night Bus
Gavin Murphy

She rubs her ticket gently so
And charts celestial bodies as they sparkle forth
Like the gentleman at the front
Revolving slow as a space station
His hat bent on a trajectory of its own,
Or the poor crathur
With rockets for pockets
And a gob full of moon spit
Spiralling out the door like a shot.

Then, peering from her coopered-oak diving bell,
She twists the plastic tube of air above her head
And voyages the depths
Catching glints of Jacques Cousteau in his metal sea flea
Heavens above.

And she swears to this day
While lying on the ocean bed
She saw a sea monster
That took three days to pass.

From Crannóg 5

Letting Go

Helena Kielty

As I slip out the side door of the church I dip my fingers in murky holy water. I'm wiping my hands along the side of my jacket as Teresa steps out in front of me. Her mousey brown hair is longer then I remember. There's a new scar on the tip of her nose and extra weight around her face.

'How are you?' she asks. The words pollute the air and I want to be away already.

'Good now' and I turn to leave but there it is; her hand on my arm.

'Do you want a hug?' her mouth, full of sunken teeth, quivers.

I don't want a hug. I stand there, motionless. Her eyes rest on me briefly and then she lunges in for an embrace. She's got as far as placing her left arm over my right shoulder before I manage to pull away.

'NO!' I shout, panicked. Images of the shower at home flash at me. I fantasise about the very hot setting, the one that pierces my skin and leaves it red and mottled for hours. I step away, recognising the familiar acid of resentfulness eat its way up my windpipe.

'Listen, I hope you're well and that everything's good and no hard feelings you did your best it just wasn't enough — no one ever gave you a manual I guess,' I say, struggling to breathe.

She moves towards me so that I'm pressed up against the wall, and thrusts a fifty euro note into my pocket.

'Do you have time for a coffee?' she asks.

I think of the Bomber flies I buy John every year for Christmas. With fifty euro I could buy seventeen of the good ones; the ones that catch the fish every time.

She grabs my arm as we cross the road and chats casually about people I went to school with. Caroline Thomason got married last month to a nice man from Drogheda. Geri Begley has three children, all boys.

The coffee shop is new and still smells of paint. 'It was a flower shop up until six months ago,' she tells me. They've managed to squash in five tall tables and some stools. The lady behind the counter looks up from cleaning and nods at us.

'Will you have something to eat?' Teresa asks.

'Just coffee.'

'I'll just have coffee too. You sure you don't want something to eat?' asks Teresa, doing that lilting thing with her voice, sounding like a child.

'No thanks, just coffee.' If the lady behind the counter's registered the change in Teresa's voice,

she doesn't let on.

'Go on, have a piece of cake,' she says, reaching into her purse to rummage at the bottom of it, her hands trembling, face slightly flushed. I remember it well; the sinking feeling in case she doesn't have enough money.

'I'll go find us a table,' I say, turning to find the table farthest from the counter so she can rummage in peace.

She arrives a few minutes later, carrying a brown tray and some of those too small white cups. She takes off her coat, revealing wet patches under her arms. The stain creeps along as she reaches for the sugar. She makes a fuss of stirring her coffee.

'So how are you?'

'I'm good,' I say.

'So, you were in with Father Shannon'

'Do you go to twelve o clock mass every day?' I ask.

'Most days,' she says, hesitantly.

'Did he tell you I was coming?'

'No. Sure he wouldn't be allowed to do that,' she says.

'He's new,' I say, carefully — aware that she wants to know how much was said to the priest but that she won't ask directly.

'Did you come back to say ten years' worth of confession?'

'I'm getting married,' I tell her quickly, 'I need the paperwork to say I've been baptised and confirmed and that I haven't been married before.'

She buckles slightly. 'That's nice love,' she says finally.

The lady at the counter fiddles about with the dials on the radio, creating white noise interspersed with snatches of various talk shows. I let my hand rest momentarily on my belly. Thirteen weeks.

'You know I'll always love you,' she says, lilting again.

'Whatever.'

'I'll always be your mam.'

'It's too late for that', I say, hearing the weariness of it. She catches my eye. My left eyelid begins to twitch, the way it always does when I'm upset and I hate that she knows it.

'So who is it you're marrying?' asks Teresa, moving momentarily to safer territory.

'His name is John,' I say, 'and he's from Kildare.'

'And are you working?' asks Teresa, glancing at my almost flat belly and then back up to my face again.

'I work with kids,' I tell her, deciding not to mention I'm a primary school teacher.

'You were always good with kids,' she says,

'any time one of the neighbours had a baby you were always there wanting to hold it.'

I nod, inhaling deeply. The shop woman uses turps to clean paint from the plastic light-switch. My nose wrinkles, remembering a similar smell from years ago.

As the men come through the door I'm standing under the counter-ledge, studying a piece of chewing gum. There are two of them, wearing woollen masks stretched across their faces. I reach gingerly for mam's glove.

'Back against the wall,' shouts the fat one.

We're the only two here, apart from the postmaster so we scramble towards the side wall. Mr Gavin holds his hands up, as though he's going to be shot, even though the men haven't any guns, they have crowbars.

'Right, empty the tills.'

Mr Gavin does as he's told, but he isn't quick enough and that makes the fat one angrier.

'Hurry the fuck up! I'm going to bleedin swing for someone!"

I stand behind mam's legs. The fat man turns to look at us. He glances at mam's face, then momentarily down to her breasts and back to her face again. He holds her gaze and smiles at her, but it isn't a friendly smile and my stomach clenches against it. The leg I'm holding begins to tremble and I cling tighter, trying to steady it. She's still holding my left hand in her glove; the wool is scratchy against my too hot hand.

'Take it. That's all the money I have. Leave us alone,' pleads Mr Gavin, but the man isn't in so much of a hurry anymore.

'What's your name darling?' he asks.

'Paddy. Jesus. Leave it.' says his friend. The fat man moves his hand behind him, as if to swat away a fly.

'I want no part in this,' says the friend.

'Just shut the fuck up and do your job.'

'Jesus,' says the friend again, looking at us nervously.

'What's your name?

Mam looks at the ground and says nothing. The man's right in her face then; there's the smell of stale chips and a faint odour of turpentine. He looks behind him to a door leading out the back.

'That's where they keep all the big parcels.' I say suddenly, wanting him to go in so we can run away.

His eyes rest on me. 'You wait here with my friend. I'm going to have a chat with your mammy in the back room for a minute,' he laughs. Mam's legs are wobbling properly, not just a little bit. She shakes her head and mumbles something he can't hear.

'What's that' he shouts, cocking his head to one side.

'No' she says louder and she starts to cry, which is what frightens me most.

'Open the door,' he says to Mr Gavin.

Mr Gavin starts shouting things, but he does as he's told.

'Take him upstairs' he says to the friend, 'and tie him to a chair or something.'

He turns back to mam, 'Come the fuck on' he barks. She shakes her head and whimpers, but doesn't move. He takes the crow bar and points it at me. 'Do you want to show me where the presents are?' he says to me, though his eyes are looking sideways at mam. I don't want to show him where they are. I squeeze mam's hand even tighter. She doesn't squeeze back. The fat man spits on the floor. He bends down to look at me. The hairs in his nose are mostly grey.

'Do you want to show me where the presents are?'

I shake my head. I wait for mam to shake her head too. I wait for her to start shouting at the man, telling him to get away from me. She doesn't actually push me towards him, she just very clearly lets go of me. The man reaches forward and takes my hand.

His friend bounds back down the stairs. 'Yer man's after pressing some warning button. Come on; we already have the bleedin money.' He rushes past the fat one and out the back door.

'Fuck it,' says the fat one, following close behind him.

Afterwards, when the men have gone and before the guards come, mam takes twenty pence from her purse and gives it to me, 'I'm sorry they grabbed you from me,' she says carefully, 'I was holding on really tightly, but they were too strong. She starts to cry. 'Isn't that what happened love? Isn't that what you've to say when they ask you?' She puts the money in my pocket.

I take a sip of the too hot coffee and it burns my lip, jerking me back.

'I blame it on you being in the intensive care unit those first few weeks,' she says suddenly. 'You hear about it now, how it interferes with bonding— but in those days, nobody thought like that.'

'What?'

'You never wanted me to hold you, not even when you were a baby; you were rejecting me even then. Do you've any idea what that's like as a mother?' Her face is blotchy now. Beads of sweat form along the bridge of her nose.

'That's total bollix and you know it,' I spit.

She looks down at the floor, 'I've no idea what you're talking about.'

'You let me go,' I say quietly, 'that day in the post-office.'

'You've always been good at exaggerating— making things up,' she says shakily.

I want to shout awful things across the table at her; the kind of things that would land like a slap and leave a permanent mark.

'I probably won't meet you again,' I say finally.

She nods. We finish our coffee in silence. I get up to go and she jerks her chair from under the table.

'Let me just go to the loo and I'll walk out with you,' she says, asking for a last few minutes.

I watch her walk towards the toilets at the back of the shop. Her navy trousers are made from that cheap synthetic material, the one you have to search hard for these days. They remind me of the navy track suit bottoms she used to wear after the post-office day; how they were stained with bits of egg or something similar. How she smelled of cornflakes and milk that's just turned and how she had a patch at the top of her head that was balding, even then. She must only be sixty two now — not old. I reach into her jacket on the back of the chair and find her purse. I put the fifty euro note and an old twenty pence piece into the front pocket and leave before she comes back.

From Crannóg 33

GrowingUp

Aoife Casby

Do you remember that summer we built
a castle on the hillside –
we shored the walls with lichened rock,
our muddy fingers put things into it
like sorrow and other deaf words.
I picked primroses, was sorry
for their delicate stems,
imagined them keening for clay
when it would have been better
to find a seed of some wild thing
and press it into the earthen garden
we built for our tiny castle.
Then we did not understand
that only picked flowers wither;
growing flowers die
and when you saw the ripped petals
I saw your eyes warble
underneath their lids
and I want to remember that,
yes,
once,
we did build
a castle
in the ribs
of a mountain.
Back then, I was able to feel
that thing when your daddy died,
a thing between fear and hunger
sitting there in places you can't touch
like in that flesh around your heart
or the season where sadness is made.

From Crannóg 8

Glaschú

Bríd Ní Chonghóile

Ag súil sráideanna Glaschú
D'airigh mé croí na ndaoine
Bholaigh mé a nádúr
agus ina a gcuid siúile stair a muintir

Ghoill muintir Glaschú orm
D'fhág siad marc orm
Thaispeáin siad dom an nádúr daonna atá caillte
Ach i réim i nGlaschú
An mbeidh mé in ann dul ar ais théis an taom a mhuscail sibh ionam?
Dhúisigh sibh mé muintir Glaschú
Agus anois airím sibh uaim.

From Crannóg 10

Novel Extract

Mike O'Halloran

We entered the function room, which was full and noisy with the accents of the whole island, and walked over to the front of the stage where the ballad group was tuning up. We stood around long enough to be noticed. Then we left and went to an upstairs meeting room where Mona Kirwan and Liam Murray were waiting. Our conversation was brief. Martin and I left the room and went down a corridor where we found the emergency exit at the back of the hotel, and then we disappeared into the night.

The rain was falling heavily and we kept our heads low as we made our way to the garage where the car was hidden. The streets were empty, and what few cars crawled by would never have recognised us; two men with their faces covered in anorak hoods on a filthy night. I started up the engine while Martin got the gun and the cartridges which were hidden down a nearby lane. He jumped into the car and said 'Let's go', as I inched out onto the track and manoeuvred the car over the laneway's bumpy surface until we came to the road that took us back up to the summit, then down the hill towards Sutton Cross. The wipers worked furiously to clear the windscreen, but I had to go slower than I wanted and I was getting more and more anxious; the darkness and the rain were conspiring to keep us invisible, but also prolonging this thing which we wanted over and done. I remember thinking a whole city began at the bottom of the hill we were descending, spread out in darkness from Howth all the way to Killiney on the far side of the crescent-shaped bay, and that tomorrow that city would awake to the news of what Martin and I had committed.

At least the man was only to be wounded. In the leg. A warning. At Sutton Cross, the lights were red. As we waited in silence for them to change green, we heard the scream of a siren and saw a yellow light flashing further down the Dublin Road. Martin swore and I tensed, but the squad car only slowed briefly as it came to the Cross, before accelerating in the direction of Howth. I breathed again. The lights changed and we took off towards the city, the line of comfortable houses on our right, the stormy bay on our left. The car, a battered old Renault 4, swayed from time to time from the sheer force of the gale blowing in from the Irish Sea; but the growing storm meant no cops on the road, checking for tax and insurance discs, and no kids out playing football on the street when we arrived at our destination. Once or twice, I glanced left and saw some of the lights of the

southside, like dull stars peering through the darkness, here and there along the coast. At the end of the bay, where the lights along the shoreline disappeared, I could make out a few faint yellow glows on higher ground, and I took what comfort I could in the fact that Killiney Hill, where we were going, was covered in the same rain-soaked darkness. I had dreaded the day I would be asked to do this, and had prayed the operation would be called off, and now, even as I drove myself and Martin towards the target, I began to hope the wreck of a car would break down, its engine spluttering to a halt somewhere along the seafront, and I could take control again of my life, which I knew, and at the same time did not want to know, I had signed over to Mona.

The Renault kept going, however, and soon we were passing through gritty Fairview with its run-down cinemas, take-away restaurants and launderettes which catered for the young civil servants and nurses living in its flats and bedsits. We crossed Annesley Bridge and the houses became grimier along the North Strand. At the corporation flats, a few faded slogans remained on the walls in support of the Hunger Strikers of '80 and '81. We came to the Five Lamps near the drug-infested Summerhill area, and had to stop. Several cars idled between us and the traffic lights.

'Shit!' It was then I saw a funeral procession of locals snaking down the hill on our right from Portland Row. Fifty or so men and women in shabby coats and worn-out shoes walked behind the hearse. Even in the rain and poor light, I could see their faces, drawn and pale. The hearse made its way onto the yellow box as the lights turned green; the cars in front of us held back in deference to the dead. I fumed. The cortege had turned into Amiens Street. It was going the same direction as us. I flung the car into gear, wanting to bypass the traffic in front and the cortege, although this was risky. 'Stop!' yelled Martin. 'They'll be turning into Sheriff Street.' And so for two minutes we crawled behind the mourners, my arms tense from gripping the wheel, my shoulders so tight they hurt me.

At last, we were moving quickly again, over the bridge and into Townsend Street, the straight run to Irishtown, and then the leafy suburbs of the southside. At Blackrock, we took the Deansgrange Road rather than go by Dun Laoghaire, where a boat from England was due and its disembarking passengers would be scrutinised by the cops. I began to fantasise that the man would not be there when we arrived, and then that I was somewhere else, anywhere else than there. I was cold and sweating, and each time I wiped the sweat from my brow, some always made its way into my eyes, causing them to sting. Martin and I had barely spoken a word since we had passed the funeral. He was less anxious than me, though he kept checking the gun was ready; putting it back on the floor, then reaching down for it and checking again. When we began the ascent up Killiney Hill I finally accepted that this was all real, that the trial runs to the southside over the previous weeks had not been for fun, and that a man was about to be shot. I began a silent prayer, my first since childhood, and, although a convinced atheist, I begged God the gun would jam or the man would not be where he was expected. Even better, we would be intercepted by the police and arrested. I would go to jail for a few years, my honour intact, and Pat Farrell would stop collaborating.

'The house is his parents', and he visits them religiously every week this time. So unless something unusual has happened, our man will be there.' Martin was telling me something we had discussed a score of times. He directed me to take a right turn and we came into an estate of comfortable bungalows which lined the hill in rows. We took another right, then a sharp left,

and Martin said, Slow down. Here, yeah, just here. Turn the car around. Quick for Christ's sake. Good.

He slipped the balaclava over his head, got out of the car, and walked briskly in the pelting rain up the short driveway. I gritted my teeth and tensed, the way I would when waiting for a dentist's injection. My foot was suspended over the accelerator. A light shone behind the curtains in the front room. An old Merc and a newer Toyota were parked in the driveway, so our man was probably there. The garden was full of shrubs; a eucalyptus tree, the biggest I had ever seen. Then the hallway was in brightness as the door opened. A millisecond pause, some kind of scuffling noise, the night-piercing crack of the gun and Martin running back to the car and flinging himself in, shouting, Get The Fuck Out of Here.

'Fuck!' he shouted again.

'What?'

'He tried to grab the gun and it went off. I think I shot him in the chest.'

From Crannóg 50

Tumble

Colette Nic Aodha

Tumble of Autumn leaves
have taken over the garden,
winter painted them a shade darker,
golden yellow of October faded,
wind is conducting a rustle-symphony
that dries the leaves and makes them fall again
but not from trees.

I wish to exchange neighbouring Poplar
for Sycamores that line your street,
sending these leaves to you
knowing I should face the elements
and clear a path to the gate.

From Crannóg 13

Seismic

Lisa Frank

I probably should have said no when he asked if he could take my shirt off. But there's something about the feeling of skin on skin that sometimes gets me to do things I shouldn't. And so just like that the shirt was off and he was straddled on top of me, his fingers manouvering his way around my body. Neck. Shoulders. Fingers inching their way further and further down my back. I closed my eyes, my breath growing heavier as he kept going, moving his fingers in circles on my skin. Around and around he went as my mind drifted slowly out of the room, through the long L-shaped hallway and into the kitchen, where I'd been arguing with my sister that morning.

'Don't ask me again,' she'd said. We were getting our breakfasts sorted. Her, tea and porridge with walnuts and sultanas. Me, coffee with a slice of cold leftover pepperoni pizza.

'Please, Jen, it would mean the world to me,' I said and handed her a spoon. I would've handed her anything to get her to give me the money.

She shook her head at me. 'If you had a proper job then you could afford it yourself and you wouldn't always have to ask me for money.'

If I had a proper job, if I had a proper boyfriend, if I had a proper life. I walked out before she could say any more.

'How's this?' he said, his voice a near-whisper as he dug hard into my shoulder blades.

I moaned, my eyes opening and closing in red-orange waves.

'Is it too hard?'

'Just stop talking,' I said.

Jen and I have always been so different, always wanted different things. I liked sex; Jen was satisfied with love. Lately she'd been setting her sights on marriage again. This time she was set on getting it right.

It was sometime last week that we were at the table folding laundry when she brought it up. 'You know you'll have to move out then,' she said. Sharing the flat with them had worked out well; but sure, I'd find something else.

'Has he proposed?' I said, though of course I knew he hadn't.

'Not yet, but he will.' She took my stack of towels and put them with hers. 'I think a May wedding would be good,' she said with a look of hope in her eyes.

And now here was Peter, asking to take off my bra. From the corner of my eye I could see him watching my reflection in the window.

'It's in the way,' he said.

I knew better, sure I knew better when he'd asked if I wanted the massage. I pushed his hands away. 'I'll do it myself.'

I could feel him watching me as I reached my arms around to the clasp.

'Turn away,' I said.

He walked out of the room and counted aloud slowly to ten. When he came back in I was back on my stomach, stripped down to my underwear.

'Well, then,' he said, 'where were we?'

Peter is alright, better than Jen's last two. Them I didn't like at all. Especially Gerry, the corporate-yes-man jellyfish who wouldn't stop yapping. *If only the economy yap yap yap. During the Celtic Tiger yap yap.* I bought a bottle of champagne the day they broke up. I drank it as I listened to Jen cry on the phone.

'Give it time, you'll find someone better,' I'd told her.

'I know,' she said with a sob, 'but I'm so tired of being alone.' It was the next week when she asked me to move in with her. I was stuck for cash so I said okay. Three weeks later she met Peter. Jen was good at getting men; it was keeping them that she had problems with. Within two months though there was talk of them moving in together and me having to leave. But Peter said the three of us living together was okay with him.

He looked at me. 'I'm fine with it if you are.'

'Did you hear that?' I said, perching up on my elbows, my head turned around and breasts in full view. I turned back around and saw Peter in the reflection. The look of fright on his face – it was priceless.

'Hear what?'

'I thought I heard something,' I said, lowering myself back down. 'Jen maybe.'

'I didn't hear anything,' he said and waited for a moment before he pushed my hair off my back.

I laughed to myself, tempted to do the Did-You-Hear-That routine again. But then he started back with the massage, his fingers slowly inching their way down the small of my back, followed by the wet lick of his tongue. After a few minutes he lowered his body on top of mine, his penis pressing hard against my thigh.

'Take off your panties,' he whispered, his lips brushing my ear, trying his best to be subtle and sultry.

I didn't say anything but as he started kissing my neck, I thought about the fight that morning. I tried to focus on that, on Jen refusing to lend me the money, saying this and that about me not having a proper job. But then my mind drifted to her talking about marriage, the sad, stupid look of hope in her eye.

I think a May wedding would be good.

I pulled away from Peter. 'It's enough now,' I said. Then I grabbed my clothes and went to my room, telling myself that this isn't who I am.

Three years later, on a tepid July afternoon, just two months after she finally got her proper diamond ring, Jen wouldn't be so lucky. There's just something about the feeling of skin on skin.

From Crannóg 41

But Still it Moves
Patrick Deeley

'But still it moves' is a phrase attributed by some to Galileo in 1633 when forced by the Roman Church to recant his claims that the Earth moves around the Sun, rather than the converse.

It moves, Galileo – the world, the universe, the billions
on billions of miles of observational space
still expanding, Edward Hubble says, and still we imagine
we are the life and soul, the one sentient hub
of the place. Still we look up, look anew – of a day
to read the weather, of a night to lose ourselves
in the hush that comes over us, call it wonderment
waiting to be met. A giant tortoise serving as a griddle
for the flat plate of the earth – not even as children
did we fancy there was that. But Ptolemy
we could picture – in our gripping of stars and planets
each to its approved spot on classroom walls
with blue-tack, or in the hoodwink of the heavens
as undeviating, before we learned how Copernicus had run
those circles in orderly courses about the sun.
You, then, never allowed out again because you dared
to let unwanted truths in; still Jupiter juggles
its moons just as you saw them, still the dance continues
after you've gone; after Newton's apple
hasn't clocked him on the head but 'occasion'd'
his notions about gravity; after Einstein has theorised
on what 'speed' can mean and 'spacetime' do;
after Hawking and co envisage tying together the job lot,
huge with miniscule, while stirring string theory
into the cosmological pot. Meanwhile, for me, this night
waits to be taken to bed. Maybe I'll dream
the twelve-ton 'Leviathan of Parsonstown' I saw today,
whose cooped pine boards – painted black –
set me thinking of a barrel to beat all barrels, our island's
once-upon-a-time world's biggest telescope,
the way it bulges at the middle as though it's gulped a deep
draught of space; dream the heavens as they shift
through its original speculum-metal eye
and how the faraway look we feel we inherit or are given to
holds us fervent, tranquil while the weight
of the world and its troubles in our watching seems to lift.

From Crannóg 45

New Moon

Joanne Dowling

'Go on,' she says, 'sure you'll be grand. Here, have another slug of this.'

Jenna holds up the drink and Mary takes a blast. She rises and heads down between the tables, trying to ignore the office crowd clapping and the tightness of the dress. She arrives at the dance-floor to the D.J., a young fellow waiting with an arranged smile. Was she mad? Most likely. But it's too late to turn back; she can't *die* in front of this lot.

The only song she remembered, the one she put down on the piece of paper, appears on a screen mounted on the stage. The *Blanket on the Ground*. Jesus, imagine having nothing but that.

Come and look out through the window.

She sees Michelle watching her from a table at the back, she who witnessed Mary's botched attempt to seduce the boss in the broom-cupboard. Or be seduced, more like. And that day, when he looked at Michelle standing at the door and she looked at him, Mary knew. In some other broom-cupboard, on some other coffee-break, they had copulated behind another supply of laundered towels. Unbeknownst to his wife, of course, who is now standing at the bar in conversation with his new secretary. Young, of course, and blonde.

'Go on Mary,' Jenna screams.

Maybe Jenna too, maybe her best friend. She turns around to read the words.

That big old moon is shining down

She remembers Jim Moran's passionate pleading words, promising that if only she would *... yes, yes that's the way ... good girl, yourself*; and his long hair and the smooth part of his skin behind the ear. Her golden knight, who took himself away to America, sending letters at first but eventually stopping. He sure put out *that* light.

The words race by, giving her the impression they are disappointed at her leaden performance.

Just because we are married.

Brian Turner is standing at the bar, taking large mouthfuls of Guinness that's leaving blobs of black and white on his upper-lip. She could marry him in the morning; if she wanted to.

Now I know you don't excite me.

The crowd laughs.

You don't know who I am.

Brian is looking at her, wiping away the stain, not smiling now.

She pirouettes to see the words but they have gone ahead, orbiting her frantic gaping, before fading into the dark. The D.J. has a bead of sweat dripping down the side of his nose and he starts to mouth the words like a demented statue. She turns away and faces the audience.

A few of the lads at the back from the factory-floor are making a bit of a rumpus, stamping feet on the wooden floor and singing *la la la* in tune with the song. Too young to know the words, too young to care.

La la la la la la la la.

She can finish it like this, if she wants to.

La la la la la la la la.

The crowd, suspecting the arrival of an ending, sing along, clapping hands and smiling. When it comes to a close, they erupt.

She walks past Jenna, laughing and waiting, Brian Turner, drinking and her boss, watching her, taking stock, but she sweeps onwards until she comes to the foyer. Finding an empty table, she takes the window-seat and looks out at the dark. She smiles to herself; this will be her last party with the company. Wherever she goes, there will always be a new moon.

From Crannóg 33

Stay in touch with

Crannóg

@

www.crannogmagazine.com

Lightning Source UK Ltd.
Milton Keynes UK
UKHW050629050321
379837UK00011B/1617

9 781907 017575